SUGAR BEE

Sugar Bee

RITA MICKLISH

Illustrations by TED LEWIN

Published by
The Trumpet Club
666 Fifth Avenue
New York, New York 10103

Text copyright © 1972 by Rita Micklish
Illustrations copyright © 1972 by Dell Publishing Co., Inc.

The Trademark Dell® is registered in the U.S. Patent and Trademark Office.
ISBN: 0-440-84599-8

Reprinted by arrangement with Dell Publishing, a division of the Bantam Doubleday Dell Publishing Group, Inc.

Printed in the United States of America
October 1988

10 9 8 7 6 5 4 3 2 1
OPM

SUGAR BEE

1

"SIT STILL, Sugar Bee!"

Sugar Bee wiggled on the edge of her chair. She picked at the cracked plastic seat and tapped her foot on the floor.

"Sit still!" her mother said again.

Sugar Bee tried. She held her head stiff while her mother pushed the pink barette into her hair and pulled the strands of hair back into a rubber band.

She wanted to leave. Even though the clock didn't work anymore she could guess what time it was, because the sun was shining in the high kitchen window. The sun only came in for a few minutes in the morning. Then it disappeared behind a tall building, leaving the room dim once again.

Her mother handed her a rumpled sack.

"Here's your lunch, Sugar Bee. Your name is on it."

Sugar Bee grabbed two books off the kitchen table. A dab of jelly stuck to one of them. She licked her finger and rubbed the spot clean. Miss Bloom, her teacher, didn't like spots on books.

Sugar Bee looked at herself in the long dull mirror before she went out. She wished she had a pink ribbon to match her barette. Her socks were baggy again and that bothered her. But they were pink and her dress was pink. That was good enough.

She didn't like her knees. Every morning she expected them to be round and smooth but they never were. They were like doorknobs and she tried to tug her dress down far enough to hide them. It didn't work. Maybe when she turned twelve, they'd change.

"Give me my kiss, Sugar Bee," her mother said, putting a hand under her chin.

Sugar Bee kissed her and gave her a hug, too. She felt like giving a hug this morning.

Then she skipped to the stairs and hopped down two by two. A fat, black baby sat in the open door of the apartment on the second floor, howling.

Outside, a lumbering garbage truck scraped the curb. Men swore and yelled as they lifted the smelly cans and dumped them. Two older girls from the basement apartment headed down the street and the men whistled. Sugar Bee smiled. One girl was pretty. Her coal black hair was brushed into a great mound. That's how her hair would be, someday.

Across the street was a sign that read, "PITTS-BURGH, CITY WITH A FUTURE." Strips of paper hung from it like noodles, curled and yellowed by the sun.

Down the street, three young boys were sitting in a cardboard box, rocking back and forth. The box tipped over and one of them cried. It was fun to play in a box if it didn't have garbage in it.

There was a new sign in the Thrift Shop window. "Black is Beautiful" it said. "Buy black." Sugar Bee pressed her nose against the glass. The Puerto Rican cook from the little restaurant was inside. She giggled. That fat lady would really have to look hard for a dress to fit.

Suddenly a car screeched its brakes. Sugar Bee turned to see if there would be a fight. People always yelled at each other when they had to stop suddenly. Sometimes, they got out of their cars and hit each other. But today nothing happened.

She walked on, dragging her toe on the cement. It sounded rough and she knew she shouldn't do it. These shoes would have to last awhile.

The traffic light wasn't working this morning. A policeman in the middle of the street was waving his right arm and blowing a whistle. When he turned toward her his badge flashed in the sun. Sugar Bee crossed slowly, so she could watch him. But he yelled to her to hurry, swinging his arm round and round and round.

A block away from school there was a spot where the sun came shining down between the buildings. She sat on the curb, enjoying its warmth. The brightness almost made her skin glow. It didn't look black and it wasn't really brown either.

Across the street, purple curtains fluttered out an open window. Sugar Bee liked purple. Once she'd had a purple skirt, when she was very young.

She scrambled up when she heard the warning bell and ran the rest of the way to school.

Sixth grade wasn't so bad. The first subject was always history. Today the class read a book about the Liberty Bell. It was a small book with pictures, passed around the room. But the period ended before Sugar Bee got her turn.

Next came English. How Miss Bloom loved English! She used up words one by one. Every word came out all rounded and neat. And she ALWAYS called the kids "Miss" or "Young Mister So and So." No other teacher ever did that.

The best thing about Miss Bloom was her clothes. She wore the brightest clothes in the whole school. There weren't even any clothes in the Thrift Shop as bright as Miss Bloom's. Her shoes were plastic with large bows or stuff that glittered. She kept a plastic flower in her hair. She wore several bracelets of different colors. Today as she wrote on the blackboard her bracelets clacked against it.

"Class! Be neat," said Miss Bloom. "Copy what I have written, and remember to BE NEAT!"

Pencils dropped here and there. Sugar Bee almost never dropped hers. It would break the point and Miss Bloom got mad if the sharpener was grinding away.

Miss Bloom paced up and down peering at every desk. Sugar Bee wiggled. She was left-handed and it was hard to write with the teacher staring down at the paper. Miss Bloom went back to her desk, tugging at her scarf and sucking at her teeth. It was a noisy habit she had. The boys were too busy writing to mimic her. Then Miss Bloom would really get mad.

"Read from your paper, if you please, Miss Stephanie."

Sugar Bee put her pencil in the desk groove. She smiled a little. She liked to be called "Stephanie." That *was* her real name, and she loved it. She stood and read what she had copied from the board:

> Silver rain drops from the sky
> Falls softly to the earth,
> As Spring tells the happy robin
> It's time for Summer's birth.

"Again, Miss Stephanie. Slowly. Read a poem with love and care."

Miss Bloom bobbed her head. The plastic flower slid out and hung over her glasses. She pushed it back.

Stephanie didn't want to read the poem again. It wasn't a true poem. Rain wasn't "silver." It was gray and ugly and it made her mother cough. Rain didn't "fall softly" either. It leaked through ceilings and made brown stains on the walls. The windows turned black around the edges when it rained. Her shoes always got soaked when it rained. Then her feet would hurt all day at school.

But Miss Bloom liked the poem. She beamed at Stephanie when she finished reading it aloud a second time.

Stephanie sat down and rolled the edge of her paper in a tight curl. Miss Bloom kept talking, about rain, about sun, about flowers and birds. And about poems and more poems.

"Poems are little pieces of the world. Someone sees the world and then writes about what he sees. That is why poems are important. They give us beautiful pieces of the world for our very own!"

Miss Bloom sighed, like an old dog does when it sleeps.

The bell rang to end the period. Stephanie frowned. Her best friend, Mary Lou Edwards, had the flu so there wouldn't be much to do at lunch time. She tried to find a sunny spot but the benches were full. She sat on the rest room steps and ate alone.

The first graders were drying paper Easter baskets. Stephanie knew some of the baskets would never hold eggs because they were too crooked. She knew she could show them how to do a better job. But little kids always whined and threw things away if they weren't finished soon enough.

She was thinking about Mary Lou, when someone stopped in front of her. She was sitting low enough to see the person's knees. They were knobby, like her own. They were Miss Bloom's knees. Miss Bloom wore a long skirt, longer than the other lady teachers. Maybe Miss Bloom wanted to hide her doorknob knees, too.

"You should chew with care, Stephanie, in order to digest your food properly."

Miss Bloom bent down toward her and her plastic flower landed in the dirt. Stephanie picked it up in a hurry, blew the dirt off and handed it back.

"Thank you, my dear. You are most polite."

Miss Bloom's brown skin was splotched like a water color painting that was too runny. Little gold pieces in her teeth twinkled when she smiled.

"You do *so* enjoy poetry, don't you, my dear? A sign of a fine mind. A sign of promise. Poems are a sign of dignity. Yes indeed, a sign of dignity."

Miss Bloom sighed again and Stephanie thought she was free to go. But Miss Bloom had more to say and rattled on and on. Stephanie didn't really care about dignity or whatever she said. She liked some poems and some she didn't like. "Silver Rain" was just a lie. She wished the bell would ring to end lunch time. She had never wished THAT before.

Miss Bloom began walking toward the building, pushing Stephanie along. Stephanie shuffled, pretending to listen. But she wanted to get her cookies out of the sack. If the bell rang now she wouldn't have time to finish them. And it rang.

Miss Bloom perked up and hurried away. So there was the whole lunch time, wasted. Not even time for cookies. Wasted.

Singing class was better, almost fun. Miss Bloom always let them pick two songs they liked best. The boys didn't really sing. They yelled. And Tommy Blue clapped his hands so hard it hurt Stephanie's ears. But singing was a good way to end the school day.

Since Mary Lou was sick, Stephanie started home alone. It was windy and her coat was too short. Maybe she could get a new one from the Thrift Shop for Easter. She hurried home. Instead of going in she waited on the steps for her mother. Her mother worked until 3:30 at the restaurant. It was not a very good job but she could eat lunch there.

She saw her mother come to the corner and wait for the light to change. Stephanie went to meet her.

A lady who lived on the floor above saw them and yelled out of her window.

"I took two eggs, Nadine. Pay you back Friday. O.K.?"

Her mother looked up and shook her head o.k. Nadine was a nice name. No one gave her mother a nickname. Even the man who collected the rent called her Mrs. Harris. Once he called Stephanie "Miss Harris" and she had grinned all afternoon.

Stephanie took hold of her mother's hand.

"Have a good day, Sugar Bee?"

"I guess so," Stephanie answered.

Everyone on the block used that silly name. Even the old woman who picked junk out of the trash cans called her Sugar Bee.

Many of the stairs sagged or were split in the middle. In the morning her mother came down the stairs quickly, but in the afternoon she always stopped on each landing. Sugar Bee could have run up the stairs just as fast as she ran down but she waited politely for her mother.

The hall was so dark that people left the yellow bulbs on all day. The lights had no glass covers. They were broken long ago and the rent man said he couldn't waste money for new ones. He was always complaining about wasting money.

"Well, Mrs. Leonard took the last two eggs," her mother said, when they went into their kitchen. She tossed the empty carton in the trash-box.

Sugar Bee went into the small room next to the kitchen. It wasn't a real room, just a corner fixed up with a sort of wall. Her narrow bed was under the window. Her fuzzy old stuffed cat leaned on the edge of the bed, faded and eyeless.

Sugar Bee changed her clothes and noticed that the tip of her shoe was loose. It looked funny inside the bottom of a shoe. She hoped it wouldn't come apart. She banged the bed against the wall.

"What are you banging in there?" her mother called from the kitchen.

"My tennis shoes were under the bed."

"Well, remember Mr. Watkins. He's still sleeping."

Mr. Watkins was an old, crippled man who lived in the apartment next door. He worked nights as a janitor and tried to sleep during the day. But there was a lot of noise when all the kids were home from school. Doors slammed, balls bounced in the halls and someone was always fighting. He would yell out of his door but the noise went on.

The four o'clock whistle blew at the pipe factory. It blew every weekday, shrill and loud. Sugar Bee wrinkled her face until it stopped.

Onions simmered in the frying pan. She sniffed. The smell bothered her but when the onions were added to the chili and beans they just got lost and didn't ruin the taste.

"Momma, can I have a piece of gum?"

Her mother looked up from the stove. She always had a piece or two in her purse.

"O.K. Just half a piece. And don't swallow it."

Sugar Bee went into the little living room and sat in the brown chair. Her mother's purse was on the floor. The clasp had broken and was kept shut with a rubber band. She found her bit of gum.

The stairs were creaking loudly and Sugar Bee knew it was her father coming home. She pushed herself against the wall next to the door. It swung open and her father came in, tossing his lunch pail in the brown chair.

"Anybody home?" he asked. "Wonder where that Sugar Bee is?"

She tried not to laugh. Her father slowly turned around with his big hands on his hips. She jumped out from behind the door.

"Whoa! It's a ghost!" her father yelled.

He grabbed her around her waist and lifted her right off her feet. Her mother came to the kitchen door and shushed them.

"You two! Remember poor Mr. Watkins." She shook her head, but she was laughing.

Sugar Bee picked up her father's lunch pail and

took it to the sink. She always opened it and rinsed it. Her father said she was his "little housekeeper" when she did it and that made her happy.

In a while she went down to the street to play. It was cold and most of the kids were inside. She didn't see Olive, her Japanese friend, who lived two apartments away.

Sugar Bee could smell suppers cooking, lots of different smells mingling together. Some smelled burnt. The old Italian widow, Mrs. Daleo, was always burning stuff on her stove. Once the fire engines came because there was smoke all over. There wasn't any fire, just old Mrs. Daleo ruining her food again.

As the sun settled somewhere across the river the clouds turned into long red ribbons. Sugar Bee wondered if clouds were always lumpy.

She heard a special whistle. Her father was leaning out of their window, whistling like a bird. He waved to her to come up to supper. She looked at the sky again. It was all gray. The rows of apartments leaned against each other, all alike. The whole world was gray.

2

AFTER SUPPER Sugar Bee dried the dishes. She could hear Mr. Watkins running his razor next door. It sounded like a bee stuck against a window.

Her father's lunch pail needed careful drying; it rusted easily. His name was painted inside with nail polish. "Carlton Harris." Sugar Bee liked that name. She liked to say it out loud. "Carlton Harris. Stephanie Harris." It looked nice.

This was the quiet time in their apartment. Her father read the paper and once in a while he would smoke a cigar. Her mother usually opened the window a little when he smoked. Sugar Bee didn't mind a cigar as much as a full ashtray. That smelled awful.

She hung up her dish towel and sat down at the kitchen table to do her homework.

"What's your assignment, Sweetie?" her mother asked. She always called it an "assignment."

"I got to read history," she said.

"You *have* to read history, Sugar Bee. Not *got*."

"Yea. I have to."

She would much rather go across the hall and watch TV at the Boltons'. They even had a roof antenna and she was always welcome. But her mother said it wasn't polite to run in and out like that.

Sugar Bee's mother stood in front of the long mirror. She wore a blue band to keep her thick hair in place. Her large eyes looked even larger, set in her thin face. Her rich brown skin was stretched tight against her high cheek bones. Sugar Bee thought she was very pretty.

"History is important," her mother said with a hairpin in her teeth.

"I don't like it," Sugar Bee answered.

"You don't like liver, either. But it makes you healthy."

"Yikkk!" Sugar Bee sputtered. "Liver is awful!"

Her mother put water in a glass and poured it

into a pot full of wide green leaves. She picked up the leaves and looked at them.

"Well, well. So you love liver. Tomorrow I'll make you a stack of juicy liver sandwiches. And some liver juice and a lot of chocolate-covered liver for recess and . . ."

Sugar Bee put her fingers around her throat and stuck out her tongue. That sounded like the worst idea ever! Her mother went in the front room and teased her more.

She said, "Honey, your little Sugar Bee wants you to run down to the store to get some nice fresh liver to eat before bed. Will you hurry up? She just can't wait."

Sugar Bee's father frowned and answered in a deep, sorrowful voice, "Liver costs a million dollars. I've only got half a million. She'll just have to wait for payday."

Sugar Bee called from the kitchen. "I wouldn't eat liver for a BUNCH of million dollars anyway!"

She was getting sleepy and cold. The stove made the kitchen a little warmer but the floor was drafty and her feet hurt. She didn't have to be told to go to bed. She put her books away and went behind her little wall.

Someone knocked on the door.

"I hope nobody wants to borrow eggs. We're all out," Mrs. Harris said as she went to answer the knock.

"Good, GOOD evening, Mrs. Harris," a voice said.

Sugar Bee jumped up. That voice was a great surprise. She stuck her feet back in her shoes and came around the wall.

In the open door stood Miss Bloom. Sugar Bee was startled. What was Miss Bloom doing here? And all dressed up in her coat with the little fur collar! (The boys at school said it was a dead cat she skinned with her teeth and sewed on her coat but Sugar Bee never believed that.)

There she was, smiling from ear to ear and shaking Mrs. Harris by the hand. Miss Bloom's bracelets rattled and her long earrings swung back and forth. Sugar Bee felt very shy. A teacher had never come to her home before. Her father got up from the chair and stood. He put out his cigar and then stood some more. Miss Bloom talked and talked and still stood in the open door.

"Won't you come in?" Mrs. Harris asked, when Miss Bloom stopped for breath.

"Why, how kind, how kind. Yes. I will, I will. Yes. Indeed!"

Miss Bloom fluttered and fussed with her coat as she stepped inside.

"This is Mr. Harris, Sugar Bee's father," her mother said.

Miss Bloom shook his hand over and over. He looked quite uncomfortable.

"Won't you sit down?" he mumbled, pointing to the brown chair. Sugar Bee quickly grabbed up the paper he had left on the seat and Miss Bloom perched in the chair.

Miss Bloom held her purse flat in her lap. It was orange plastic with a chain handle and matched her orange shoes. The plastic flower in her hair was also orange.

Sugar Bee stood in the kitchen doorway. Her mother and father sat on the two plastic chairs and that's all there were. She didn't mind standing because she was excited that Miss Bloom was really there. She stared at the rip in the arm of the brown chair. Maybe Miss Bloom wouldn't see it. The chair seemed so dingy compared with the bright Miss Bloom.

". . . and she is such a fine, fine student!" Miss Bloom was saying.

"We're pleased to hear that," Mrs. Harris said quietly.

"Yea. She studies easy," said Mr. Harris. He still looked uncomfortable.

"I have come on a very special errand," Miss Bloom said, each word chopped off neat as could be. She leaned forward, squashing her orange purse in her lap.

"Is there trouble at school?" Sugar Bee's mother asked in a puzzled voice.

"Oh dear me! Dear me, no. No in-deed!" Miss Bloom always used "indeed" in two parts. "In . . . deed."

Miss Bloom wiggled a bit in the brown chair, then sat stiff.

"I have a very special invitation for your daughter."

"An invitation?" Mrs. Harris asked. She looked at her husband.

"Yes. A once-in-a-lifetime invitation, I do believe," Miss Bloom beamed.

Sugar Bee had been looking at the floor. She noticed the big cracks in the wood, near the corner. But Miss Bloom wasn't turned that way. She wouldn't see them from the brown chair, thank heavens. But she would see the light in the ceiling. All around the light the plaster had fallen away. When the people upstairs thumped the floor, more plaster fell down. The wood pieces and black wire showed in the hole. Sugar Bee hoped the people upstairs wouldn't thump the floor while Miss Bloom was there. The far corner of the wall was stained where rain leaked in and it had puffed and split.

Sugar Bee had never noticed so many broken spotted things in the room before. Now they leaped out at her. The edge of the door was splintered where a dog had chewed it, and there were mouse holes along the baseboards. The cold cigar in the ashtray was smelling up the whole room.

Sugar Bee kept a worried eye on Miss Bloom but the teacher didn't look around. She was too busy explaining something to her parents. They were nodding and trying to smile. Finally Miss Bloom stopped speaking and Sugar Bee hoped she wouldn't look at the ceiling, or the floor, or even at the arm of the chair.

"That's a kind invitation," her mother was saying.

Suddenly Sugar Bee realized she hadn't heard a word they had said. She had been too busy worrying about the room.

"We'll try and work it out. But we can't really

say . . . right now." Her mother spoke softly and she seemed troubled.

"I'm sure your decision will be correct. And this young lady will be thrilled," Miss Bloom said. She stood up so quickly Sugar Bee thought something had poked her.

"I must go. Must go. My school work takes much of my evenings, too. Yes. I must." Miss Bloom stepped over to Sugar Bee and patted her on the head.

"Yes, yes, Stephanie. You will be thrilled!" Her many bracelets knocked against Sugar Bee's head.

Then she was gone. Her mother was strangely quiet. She didn't talk about the visit as she would if a neighbor had come in. Her father sank deep in the brown chair reading the paper. They didn't even talk to each other.

Sugar Bee felt stupid. She had to find out why Miss Bloom came, but she was too embarrassed to ask.

She got ready for bed and crawled under her covers, worried. She thought about the living room. Why had it looked so bad? The holes in the curtains, streaks on the walls, the brown chair. *It* bothered her most. And it was the only real chair they had.

Miss Bloom had looked so bright. The flower seemed to pop right out of her hair. And all her clothes matched.

The neon light across the street flashed through the kitchen window. Shadows made her bed red, green, red, green.

Sugar Bee remembered how Miss Bloom had patted her head and called her "Stephanie." She hoped her mother heard that. Her mother came around the wall and sat on the bed. "You forgot to undo your hair, Sugar Bee," she said. She unwound the rubber band and loosened Sugar Bee's hair very gently. If Sugar Bee was going to find out about the visit, she knew she had better do it now.

"Gee, Miss Bloom sure surprised me," she said.

"Me, too," her mother whispered.

"Isn't she . . ." Sugar Bee was going to say pretty. But Miss Bloom wasn't pretty. She was too skinny. She had a long face like you see in the side of a coffee pot.

"Miss Bloom is very bright, isn't she?" Sugar Bee asked.

"Bright? You mean her clothes?" Her mother tucked the blanket around the bottom of the mattress.

"Uhuh," Sugar Bee said sleepily.

"Oh yes. She's very bright and very kind." Her mother bent close to her.

"She likes poems a lot."

"She likes *you* a lot," her mother answered. "That's why she came herself to tell us about the invitation."

Sugar Bee raised up on her elbow.

"Momma, I didn't hear what she said."

"You didn't hear her? Why, you were almost standing on top of her! How come you didn't hear?"

Sugar Bee just couldn't talk about the ugliness of the walls or the floor or the brown chair. It wasn't her mother's fault that the room was so awful.

So she whispered, "I just didn't listen."

Her mother wiggled her head by lightly tugging on her hair.

"Silly one. Your own teacher sits in our front room and you don't listen to her. Not even about the invitation?"

"No," Sugar Bee said in a guilty voice.

"Well, no wonder you didn't say thank you when she left! She came to invite you some place wonderful—"

Sugar Bee grabbed her mother's hand. "A party?" she squealed.

"Shush!" Her mother shoved her under the blankets. "Miss Bloom has to choose someone from your class to go away during Easter vacation to a . . ."

"Did she choose me? Did she?"

"She'd *like* to choose you, honey. But . . ." Her mother paused. Sugar Bee almost didn't breathe.

". . . but it would cost some money. And . . . there just might not be any money for that," her mother said very slowly.

Sugar Bee lay as still as she could. She wanted her mother to go on, to say that there WOULD be money. To say that Miss Bloom could really, truly choose her. She wanted so much to hear her mother say it. But her mother stood up. The flashing neon light made her face look sick and tired.

"We have to think about it. Your poppa has to see what he can do." She bent to kiss Sugar Bee.

"Do you understand?"

Sugar Bee tried to answer but all her words got mixed up and wouldn't come out. She DID understand about money. It changed a lot of things. It always did. But she hoped it wouldn't change this.

"Goodnight, honey." Her mother left.

Sugar Bee didn't cry. She just began to think about Miss Bloom and about being chosen to go.

She didn't even know WHERE she would go if she was chosen. That didn't matter. If only she COULD be chosen.

After Sugar Bee fell asleep, her parents sat on their bed in the dark for a long time.

"That teacher is sure partial to orange, huh?" Sugar Bee's father mumbled.

"The kids like it. The brighter the better, I guess."

They were silent.

"Sugar Bee deserves to go. She really deserves it," Mrs. Harris said quietly.

"Yea. You bet she does. She's smart." Mr. Harris pounded his pillow flatter.

"And she needs it, Carlton. She needs something fine like that. Something good and even pretty." Mrs. Harris seemed to choke a little. She coughed softly.

"Pretty?" Mr. Harris asked.

"Yes, pretty. She needs something pretty; girls need it."

"Well, Nadine, maybe it wouldn't be a good idea to give her something for a little while and then take it away."

Mrs. Harris touched his shoulder.

"If she got to see something special, *do* something special, nobody could take it away from her. She could always remember."

The next morning Sugar Bee stayed curled in bed. She knew it was time to get up but she didn't. Not right away. Miss Bloom's visit didn't turn into a dream, like Christmas or birthdays did. She could have a dozen dreams about Christmas, a dozen adventures in her head as pretty and exciting as she wanted. No dream came about Miss Bloom. Only questions now, filling her head in the early morning. Questions and worry. What kind of invitation? Not a party, her mother had said. Going somewhere. Going away. Where? Why? And *when* would it be, if it ever did happen? How come Miss Bloom brought this "invitation"? A teacher?

Sugar Bee felt her excitement rise again and she curled tighter in the bed. Then she remembered the rest of it. Her mother's face in the darkness. Sad. Worried. Tired. And the money. The darned old money!

She looked at the ceiling above her bed. It was just as awful as the front room. What was the matter with everything? Holes in the wall covered with tape never bothered her before. Now they did.

Even her blanket was ragged. Her pink dress hung crooked on the wall. Yesterday it was all right. Today it wasn't.

"It's late, Sugar Bee. Breakfast is ready," her mother said, leaning around the wall. Her mother didn't sound or look sad, like last night.

"Maybe they decided about the money and I can go," Sugar Bee thought.

She slid out of bed and pulled on her dress. It wasn't such a bad dress. She smoothed the skirt, tied the belt and hurried to the table. Her father was leaving for work.

"Hey, Sugar BeeBee!" Sometimes he used two Bees. "On the way home I'll get you that liver you love. For some de-lish-ous liver sandwiches. O.K.?"

Sugar Bee laughed. "O.K. But I won't eat it anyway, for a million more dollars. I won't!"

He threw her a kiss. He looked very fine in his work jacket. It said "Central Pipe Supply" in red letters on the back. The truck he drove said the same thing in the same kind of giant letters.

Her mother dressed for work while Sugar Bee ate. She rinsed the bowl with water so the cockroaches wouldn't swarm all over by afternoon. Her mother gave her a hurried look.

"Come on. We'll both be late."

"Momma, did you and Poppa decide?" Sugar Bee was all ready to smile.

"Decide what?" her mother asked, slipping into her coat.

"About the invitation." Sugar Bee had all her questions crammed in her head, waiting for good answers.

"Oh." Her mother looked at her. "Not yet, honey. Poppa said we'll have to wait and see."

Sugar Bee turned away. It was just the same. Nothing had changed since last night. She picked up her books and coat and went down the stairs, slowly.

Black, brooding clouds hung above the city, heavy with rain. Sugar Bee frowned at them. When she was younger, someone had told her that if she jumped high enough, she could stick clouds with a pin and the rain would all leak out of the hole she made. It was dumb, but she used to believe it.

At the corner some boys were shoving each other. She stopped. It was the beginning of a fight. There were black boys and white boys. One boy fell, slipping into the gutter. Another boy jumped down on him, slamming his fists and feet. All the boys shouted dirty hate words.

Sugar Bee pressed flat against the brick wall. Fights terrified her.

The fight was right in front of the little grocery store. The gaunt Chinese man who owned the store ran out, waving a long push broom over his head. He started hitting the fighters with it. The other boys shoved him aside, yelling.

"Beat it, old man, get out! Get out!"

He stumbled back into his store and slammed the door shut. Sugar Bee heard sirens. Police cars were coming. The boys broke and ran, all of them.

Sugar Bee ran, too, to get away from the noise and dirty words. She darted across the street without even looking for traffic. She had seen fights before, too many of them. Today she didn't think she could stand anything else being wrong.

After two blocks, she stopped running.

3

IT BEGAN to rain. It was a drizzle at first and Sugar Bee poked along. She didn't care if she got wet or not. In the middle of the last block it really poured and she had to run. The kids were all pushing around the doors trying to get in first. Safety Patrol boys came from the street corners, their yellow coats slick and dripping.

Sugar Bee stamped her wet feet. In the cold drafty school, they would hurt all day. She could see rain sliding over the glass windows in the long school hall. It sure wasn't "silver" stuff. She hated it.

In class she didn't look around to see if Mary Lou had come to school today. She didn't look at anybody. Even before class began she wanted to go home. If she stayed she would have to see Miss Bloom and she just couldn't! She tried to make herself feel sick or hot so the teacher would think she had the flu. But her hands were icy cold, not hot with fever.

The bell rang and she was stuck. In came Miss Bloom wearing the same orange shoes she had on last night. She began to write on the board—poems, poems, poems.

The rest of the class began to copy. Sugar Bee just sat. Miss Bloom didn't notice. Three pictures leaned against her desk, trees in bloom, horses in a pasture and a girl sitting beside a stream. Each picture had a poem and Miss Bloom was reciting them. Sugar Bee stared at the window. Gray gloomy squares.

Quickly the morning passed and lunch time was spent inside. The boys yelled about it. They would rather go out and get soaked, just for fun. She took out her lunch sack and remembered what her father had said about liver. She smiled a tiny bit.

One of the boys grabbed her apple and tossed it to another boy. She didn't even try to stop them. They wanted to tease her and make her angry. But she just turned her back to them. Some kids rolled marbles on the floor, others scribbled on the board.

Sugar Bee looked sourly at every inch of the classroom. Big posters hung on the back wall but they just covered cracks. The lights were dusty and yellowed. The desks were cut and scarred. She didn't understand why she noticed all of this now. She had been in the room for the whole school year and never cared about the beat up things. Why did they make her so unhappy today?

All day she worried about it. She saw things in a different way. Everything had something wrong with it. Nothing in the whole school was really new or good. Even the American flag above the statue of George Washington at the end of the hall was ragged and faded.

When the final bell rang Sugar Bee grabbed up her books in a great hurry and pushed her way out the front door. She almost never pushed her way through, but she wanted to get away from there!

"Stephanie! Stephanie!" someone called.

It was Miss Bloom. Sugar Bee put her head way down and shoved. She pretended she didn't hear anything, and hurried into the crowd of other children.

Her shoes had almost dried but she walked in water on purpose. She was sad and angry, then sad again. The cars splashed dirty water from the gutter. It made oily streaks and rainbow stains on the sidewalk. She slipped and almost fell.

A buggy was parked outside the market with a white baby in it sucking a pacifier. Sugar Bee didn't even smile at it and she loved babies.

The Thrift Shop was full of people. She saw Olive and her tiny mother. Any other day she would have asked Olive to play. Today she just glanced in and hurried on. She probably wouldn't even get a coat there for Easter. She'd probably have to wear the same short, awful one.

She ran up the stairs, went into the apartment and slammed the door. Mr. Watkins woke up and thumped on the wall. She didn't care. Sugar Bee flopped on her bed and kicked off her wet shoes. She rubbed her cold, hurting feet. She hadn't waited for her mother. She didn't care about that either.

Now she heard her coming. It seemed to take her a long time to climb the stairs. Mrs. Harris came in quietly, closing the door with care. She would never disturb a neighbor who was trying to sleep. Sugar Bee was sorry now that she had slammed the door. It was mean.

She heard her mother sit on her own bed and change shoes. Her slippers made a soft slap-slap on the bare wood floors, as she came around the wall.

"Hi, honey. You must have run all the way home."

Sugar Bee didn't look up. She kept rubbing her cold feet.

"Your shoes are soaked again. They'll fall apart if you don't keep out of puddles."

"Yea," Sugar Bee mumbled.

Her mother started coffee and the smell soon filled the apartment. Sugar Bee moved to the stove, heating her hands and rubbing her feet again. Her mother held the steaming cup and let it warm her fingers.

"Slow day today," her mother said as she sipped the coffee.

"Cause it rained," Sugar Bee said. Rain slowed restaurant business.

They sat thinking to themselves. As more rain fell Sugar Bee frowned at the messy ceiling. Would the whole thing swell up from rain, maybe even fall apart?

She said out loud, "It's ugly!"

Her mother looked right at her. "What, Sugar Bee?"

Sugar Bee sat and pouted.

"What did you say, honey?"

"It's . . . ugly!" Sugar Bee said almost under her breath.

"What's ugly?" her mother asked, putting down her cup.

"Everything!" Sugar Bee said it loud.

"Since when is everything ugly, Sugar Bee?"

Sugar Bee frowned at her mother. She had a lot of answers to that question but she didn't know how to use them. Her mother stared at her, making her squirm.

"This room is ugly. And so is the front room. Everything we have is ugly."

It wasn't nice to look at her mother like that. She could feel that it was wrong but she was so very unhappy. She didn't know what else to do. She wanted to cry but it didn't happen. Her mother rinsed her cup, leaned against the sink and stared at the ceiling, too. Sugar Bee bit her lip and slid down in the chair.

There were tears on her mother's face. She hadn't seen her mother cry since her little brother had died and that was a long time ago. Sugar Bee was ready to cry now, too.

"Poor Sugar Bee baby. You have to learn about ugly things someday. We all have to."

Her mother went to the window and made little circles on the steamy glass.

"You know we aren't rich people, Sugar Bee. We have to use what we have. We have to use everything until it just won't work anymore. Even this apartment. It has to be used until it's all worn out. And we have to stay. We can't have anything better, not yet. Maybe someday, before too long. . . ."

The factory whistle sounded softer in the rain. Sugar Bee and her mother said no more. They were both sad as they waited for Sugar Bee's father.

He was whistling when he opened the door. His jacket had beads of rain on it and his hair was damp. Sugar Bee sat in the kitchen. She didn't pick up his lunch pail.

Her father said in a big voice, "Hey, come see what I got for girls who love liver!"

He rustled a paper bag in the air. Sugar Bee slowly went into the front room. He sat in the torn brown chair, the sack on his knee. He stuck his hand in, pretending to find something.

"There she is, the gal who dreams about liver sandwiches. Come on over here. It's the best liver you can buy. Only half a million dollars. Some bargain, huh?"

Her father was laughing while he played his little game and she couldn't even smile.

"Well, what do ya know? No liver in here, must have slipped out of the bag! Not even one drippy, juicy piece. Ain't that a shame?"

He held out a pack of cinnamon gum, her favorite kind.

"How about this instead, Sugar Bee Bee?"

She took the gum with a very quiet "thank you."

"Is the coffee hot?" he asked his wife. He stretched his long arms and went into the kitchen. Mrs. Harris poured him a full cup. Sugar Bee leaned on the doorway, feeling uneasy. She knew she had been unkind to her father by not playing the game about liver. They ate dinner, hamburgers and green beans. Sugar Bee ate all the beans even though she didn't like them. Her conscience hurt. Her father was talking about one company truck that lost its brakes in the rain and hit a bridge. Sugar Bee didn't listen very much. She tried to keep her eyes down. She didn't want to see the junk around her, broken junk.

Her father pushed his chair back.

"Did you see that Miss Bloom today?" he asked suddenly.

Sugar Bee jumped a little. The question scared

her. She quickly remembered how she ran away from Miss Bloom after school. It was the wrong thing to do. Her parents wouldn't like that.

She answered softly, "Yes."

"She sure is a nice lady. Don't you think?" her father asked.

Sugar Bee nodded. She saw her mother's eyes get sad again.

"She thinks a great deal of you."

Again Sugar Bee nodded.

"It made us real proud to hear your teacher bragging about you, Sugar Bee. Real proud." Her father smiled at her.

He reached in his shirt pocket and took out a small envelope. He put it in the middle of the table and tapped it with his finger. Sugar Bee's mother looked puzzled. She watched that envelope like it might get up and walk all by itself.

"Miss Bloom is sure you have a good mind, to learn and study. She even thinks you might write poems someday. Maybe you do it already. Do you, Sugar Bee?" he asked.

"Some little ones, not much," she said with a small smile.

"Momma said you didn't understand what Miss Bloom came about. It's real special. She wants you to go to the country for a whole week during your Easter vacation."

Her father kept tapping the envelope. Sugar Bee stared at it and so did her mother.

"Momma and I talked about you going to the country. It's a fine chance, Sugar Bee. We wanted to say yes to Miss Bloom but . . ." he paused.

Sugar Bee felt the tears coming. She knew. They had to decide and there wasn't ever enough money.

Her father went on, carefully.

"But I couldn't say yes. Not right away. I had to do some thinking and see about the money you'd need."

He pushed the envelope toward her.

"I got the money for you, Sugar Bee. It's in there. You tell Miss Bloom it's o.k. You can go."

Her mother put her arms around her father and kissed his cheek. She didn't say anything but that was all right. Sugar Bee stared at the envelope. It was decided. She could go. She could go!

4

A LARGE CALENDAR hung next to the stove. It read "Central Pipe Supply" above a picture of many trucks in a row. A man stood beside each truck and way down the line was Mr. Harris. It was hard to tell which one he was but Sugar Bee was very proud of the picture and had taken it to school right after Christmas to show her friends.

She made another crayon mark. Five days until Easter vacation. But now it was school time and she grabbed her lunch and ran. In the street she waved up to her mother.

"Remember," her mother called from the window. "We go to the Thrift Shop right after school. Hurry home!"

"I will!" she yelled back as she ran. They were

going to look for a dress to wear when she went away. She wouldn't be late for anything like that!

In school Mary Lou followed her everywhere. Ever since Miss Bloom had told the class about Sugar Bee's invitation, Mary Lou had stuck to her like glue. Today Miss Bloom would have the "details" as she called it.

"What if something happens? What if . . ." Mary Lou jabbered with a long face.

"It won't!" Sugar Bee said, a little snappy.

"Maybe your father'll say no, change his mind. . . ."

"Nope! He wouldn't do that. He got the money and Momma's getting me a dress." She wished Mary Lou would shut up for once.

"Yea? What kinda dress do you want?"

Sugar Bee knew exactly what dress she wanted. She'd seen it in a magazine. It was a long-sleeved yellow dress with ruffles at the neck and wrist. The girl in the magazine wore yellow shoes and white gloves and had shining blond hair. Sugar Bee wistfully smoothed her thick black hair. She would look fine in a yellow dress like that, but she knew she'd never get it. The girl in the picture was white and must be rich. Her mother would just look at everything in the Thrift Shop and pick one out that fit.

It was time for English. Miss Bloom stood before the class stiff as a board. She held up a letter.

"Class, you all know an outstanding student has been invited to spend Easter week away." She made the word echo in the dingy old room. Sugar Bee shivered.

"In the country." Miss Bloom smiled a radiant smile, all her teeth sparkling.

Mary Lou squealed. "The countryyyyyy!"

"Yes, in the country, where Spring is gay and colorful," Miss Bloom said in her best poem voice.

Sugar Bee had her arms wrapped all the way around her middle. Where? Where? Where? She almost jumped up and shouted the question. Miss Bloom turned and wrote slowly on the board.

"Dr. and Mrs. R. Martin and daughter.

Morningside Way, Red Ridge, Penn."

Sugar Bee stared at the board. This was the place. This was the family. She was going to Red Ridge! To Red Ridge!

After school Miss Bloom told Sugar Bee to follow her to the Principal's Office. They went right into the room marked "Private." Mr. Goodstead, a little man with a gray mustache and a nice smile, sat in a creaky high-backed chair behind a littered desk.

"Your parents are expecting this letter, Stephanie. It is information about your host family. Learn all you can from your visit. Perhaps Miss Bloom will invite me to your class when you're back and you can tell us about it."

Sugar Bee nodded and tried to smile. But she was nervous about being in that office, even though she wasn't being scolded. Miss Bloom led her out and patted her head.

"Now. Straight home. Don't dawdle. Take great care of that letter." She paused and blinked her eyes.

"I am very happy for you, Stephanie."

Sugar Bee looked right at Miss Bloom. Were those tears? Miss Bloom couldn't be crying. Teachers didn't cry.

Suddenly Sugar Bee remembered about the Thrift Shop. Oh boy, her mother would be waiting. She ran down the hall and bounded off the steps. Sitting there in an impatient, sloppy heap was Mary Lou.

"Sugar Beeee . . ." Mary Lou screeched, "What happened in the Office?"

Sugar Bee almost paused but instead she headed for the corner. Mary Lou was at her heels.

"I got a letter from Mr. Goodstead," Sugar Bee said, wiggling it toward Mary Lou for a second. She was jumping on her toes, impatient for the light to change.

"What about, what about?" Mary Lou yanked on her sleeve.

"Let go. I gotta go. I gotta get home!" Sugar Bee snapped.

Mary Lou dropped her hand and her eyes filled with tears as fast as she could blink. Her mouth tightened and all at once her fat brown cheeks were streaked with tears. Sugar Bee glared at her. What a dumb thing to do. Just because she was in a hurry for something *important*, dumb old Mary Lou starts to cry!

The light changed and cars rumbled past, but Sugar Bee didn't cross. She pulled Mary Lou by the sweater and stood against the sagging school wire fence.

"Don't cry!" Sugar Bee ordered. She sounded mad but she was really worried. No one likes to see her best friend cry. She held out the letter very carefully so Mary Lou could see it, the whole thing.

"Look. It's for my folks. It's closed, see? It's important. But I gotta go right now, cause Momma is waiting. She's going to get me my dress."

Mary Lou rubbed her nose and sniffed. Sugar Bee started to the corner again.

"Listen," she said, coming back to Mary Lou. "You ask your mother to let you stay over tonight, o.k.? My momma will say you can. Your brother can bring you."

She waved the envelope in the air and ran across the street. She yelled back to Mary Lou, "You ask, o.k." Then she ran down the sidewalk, dodging people and dogs. She was late!

The bell over the Thrift Shop door plink-plinked when the door opened. Sugar Bee ran inside. Her mother was at the back of the shop looking through dresses hung on metal pipe racks. Behind a low counter Gloria was brushing a man's hat. Different people took turns operating the shop and Gloria was Sugar Bee's favorite. She was quite beautiful. Her marvelous skin gleamed and her hair was high and full, almost an ebony crown. She wore long wispy dresses that floated around her. She waved her slender hand at Sugar Bee and flashed a brilliant smile.

Mrs. Harris called to Sugar Bee impatiently. "You picked a poor day to be late. I got off work half an hour early so we could look through here. Where were you?"

Sugar Bee held out the envelope from Mr. Goodstead. It was crumpled because she had held it so tightly. Her mother opened it carefully.

"The Principal sent it to you and Poppa. I had to go to the office. But I ran home, all the way." Sugar Bee was still panting.

Her mother pulled gently on her nose.

"All right, my Miss Harris. I'm not mad. I'm glad to get this letter. Did you know it tells us who you'll stay with?"

Sugar Bee nodded her head. She knew the name by heart. Dr. and Mrs. Martin and daughter. And that wonderful place—Red Ridge.

Gloria came back with a stack of hats for a shelf.

"Can I give you a hand, Nadine? I know what's where."

Mrs. Harris nodded and the two of them kept looking. Gloria held up a dress. It was yellow, with long sleeves! Sugar Bee wiggled her way past some cartons and took the dress.

"Look, Momma!" she bubbled.

Her mother held it up against her. "Ummm—way too small."

Sugar Bee ran her hand over the skirt. It was too small. How she wished it was bigger. Her mother held out another dress, white with little daisies all over. There was a ragged little cutout daisy on the collar and only two buttons left. It was big enough. Her mother took her behind a screen to try it on. Gloria came around to see.

"Hey, that's nice. A little short but you can let it down." Sugar Bee frowned. She hoped her mother wouldn't decide to let the hem down. That would leave a mark on this special dress, her country dress.

She took the dress off and Gloria put it in a used sack. They went to the counter. Sugar Bee liked to watch the cash register open. It was big and very old and it made a fine sound when the drawer slid out. Gloria held the money in her hands, her long nails curving over it.

"Hear your baby's going away," she said with a strange look in her eye.

Mrs. Harris said, "Yes, that's right. She was chosen from the whole school."

Sugar Bee felt embarrassed to hear her mother bragging about her.

"For a whole week, huh? In the country? That's a long way from home. A long way from a lot of things." She kept running her nails over the money while she talked.

Mrs. Harris picked up the package, and she seemed uneasy.

"Sugar Bee is eleven and she'll learn a lot. Won't you, honey?" Her mother touched her face. Sugar Bee wondered why she looked worried.

"Charity is tough to chew and hard to swallow, especially for kids," Gloria said, and she shut the cash register drawer very hard.

"No! Not charity, Gloria," Mrs. Harris said quickly. Her voice had turned harsh. "Sugar Bee *earned* this trip. Earned it by being an 'outstanding student.' She was chosen by her teacher. And we couldn't be more proud of her." Mrs. Harris took Sugar Bee's hand and they went to the door.

"Thanks for your help. Have a nice day," Mrs. Harris said to Gloria and they left, the little bell plinking behind them.

That evening Sugar Bee washed and dried the dishes so her mother could fix the dress. The hem had to come down and there was a faded line that cut across the daisy pattern. There were new green buttons and they looked pretty.

Mr. Harris read the letter from Mr. Goodstead and lit his cigar. The smoke made the room swirled and spooky.

"Try this on now," her mother said.

Sugar Bee went to her nook and put on the new dress. The buckle on the belt was shiny. She even put on her school shoes. Now she noticed how scraped the toes were. She was sorry now that she'd dragged her feet on the sidewalks. The scuffed shoes looked awful with her nice dress. She went slowly back into the front room, and stood still, hoping her father wanted to see her.

Mr. Harris looked up from his paper.

"Say, Momma, look at that flower garden. There's daisies all over this room."

Sugar Bee smiled like Miss Bloom did when she was ready to read a poem.

"You rub a good shine on those shoes of yours and you'll be pretty as a picture, Sugar Bee Bee," her father nodded.

Sugar Bee hung the dress up, and sat looking at her shoes. Why was something always ugly? Why couldn't something be all pretty for once?

It was very late. She took one more look at the calendar on the wall. In the morning she could

make another mark and be another day closer to
her wonderful vacation. She wanted morning to
come quickly. But just as she crawled into bed
there was a banging on the front door. A loud
gravelly voice boomed through the apartment. It
was Mary Lou's brother, Reuben. He had the
loudest voice in the world. Maybe it was because
he was almost the fattest person in the whole
world. Sugar Bee tugged her school dress back on
and ran barefoot to the front room. Mary Lou was
trying to squeeze past her huge brother and come
through the door. Reuben filled the space like a
balloon blown up too far.

"I brought ya the brat," he bellowed.

Mr. Harris grinned. "Hey Reuben, how ya
been? You're looking poorly, losing too much
weight. Better get you some good food."

Suddenly Sugar Bee remembered. She'd forgotten to ask her mother if Mary Lou could stay.

"Momma, I forgot cause we went to get the
dress. And I told Mary Lou to ask her mother if
. . ." Sugar Bee rattled away.

"It's all right. She's welcome. But it's late so
both of you get to bed," Mrs. Harris said.

Mary Lou had her pajamas in a sack. They went
to the nook.

"Momma almost didn't let me come. She was

mad at Reuben. He broke another chair," Mary Lou giggled.

Sugar Bee rolled back on the bed and laughed. Once she had seen Reuben squash a chair into a dozen pieces. It was the funniest thing ever. Reuben could sure mess up a chair.

Sugar Bee remembered her new dress. She told Mary Lou to shut her eyes and not peek. She put it on and held the skirt out just like in the magazines.

Mary Lou said, "Gee, it's real nice." Then she pointed her nose in the air and said, "but I don't like your shoes."

Sugar Bee glanced down. She was barefoot.

They started to giggle again and kept it up until Mrs. Harris turned out all the lights. It was lumpy in the little bed, one of them at each end.

"Where is Red Ridge?" Mary Lou whispered.

"Poppa said it's almost two hundred miles in the country where they have farms and stuff."

"Are you going to fly on a jet?"

"Who me?" Sugar Bee sat up. "I don't want to go on no jet. Poppa says I'll go on a bus."

"A bus? To go two hundred miles?" Mary Lou was surprised. "You'll be scared."

"I will NOT." Sugar Bee rolled up in a ball

under the covers. She had already told herself that she wouldn't be scared.

"What if you can't ever come back?" Mary Lou whispered, like someone in a scarey movie.

"Don't be dumb," Sugar Bee hissed at her. "I get to stay a week and then come home."

"Maybe they won't like you. Maybe they'll lock you up or something." Mary Lou loved to shiver and talk about creepy things.

Sugar Bee was almost sorry she had bothered to ask Mary Lou to stay. She had a lot of pretty plans to make and nice things to think about for the trip. Mary Lou was ruining everything.

"My mother'll get Maudie to tell your fortune. Then you'll *know* if something awful is going to happen," Mary Lou kept up.

The shadow of Mary Lou perched at the end of the bed gave Sugar Bee some shivers of her own. She knew about Maudie, a wicked, wrinkled old black woman who peered at people's hands and yelled like a witch. Sugar Bee kept her own hands pinched up tight.

"I'm not letting any old witch touch me. She's nutty. And *you* better stop talking like that or I won't tell you *anything* about Red Ridge when I get back," Sugar Bee hissed angrily.

Mary Lou scooted under her end of the covers and it was quiet.

"I wish I could go with you," Mary Lou whispered.

Sugar Bee didn't answer. It would be nice to have a friend along on such a special trip. She wasn't scared to go alone. Not really, she told herself. But it would be nice if . . . She closed her eyes.

There was a girl. Miss Bloom had said "Dr. and Mrs. Martin and daughter." But what was she like? Sugar Bee tried to make a picture of this girl in her head but it didn't work.

Something else bothered her. Why had Gloria at the Thrift Shop been so strange? What did that beautiful young woman mean about charity? She had earned this trip like her mother said. Why did anyone find things wrong with it? Why couldn't they just let her alone, let it be all good.

Half dreaming, Sugar Bee made her own plans. She made a picture of that wonderful place called Red Ridge and a picture of that other girl. She fell asleep trying.

When he was sure the two girls were asleep, Mr. Harris rubbed his face hard and sat on the edge of the sagging bed.

"What are you goin' to tell Sugar Bee about the girl, Nadine?" he asked his wife.

"What girl?" she answered in a sleepy voice.

He took a deep breath. "The Martin girl."

"Nothing!" His wife answered. Her voice was low but sharp.

"Honey, Sugar Bee's gotta know—"

"No, Carlton. She isn't going to know. I don't want her to know."

"Look. Sugar Bee's going to find out when she gets there." Mr. Harris tried to keep his voice down.

"And that's soon enough. Right now everything is perfect. She's happy. She's just busting with dreams about all of this. I *won't* spoil it. If we tell her she'll be disappointed. I'm sure it'll be all right once she's met the girl."

Mr. Harris sat with his head in his hands.

"I don't know, Honey. It'll be a shock. But I hope you're right."

5

ALL THE MARKS were made on the calendar. The waiting was over, for Saturday morning had come. It was still dark when Sugar Bee was awakened by her mother.

"Sugar Bee, it's time to get ready."

A few moments passed before Sugar Bee realized this was the day. She jumped up.

"Is poppa awake? Is he ready to go? Do we have to eat breakfast?" She asked questions so fast her mother had to shush her.

"We have plenty of time to eat, don't worry. Poppa is almost ready. We're just waiting for you, sleepyhead."

Sugar Bee ate as quickly as she could but the food didn't go down easily. She had a lump in her throat and she kept looking at the calendar. It was marked right up to this very day. This day!

Her father came in with the little gray suitcase he had borrowed from Mr. Watkins next door. Everything Sugar Bee owned was in it. She jumped up and took it from him, she wanted to carry it all the way to the bus station. Her mother put on her coat. They were ready.

They tried not to make any noise as they went down the stairs, but the old boards creaked and groaned. Sugar Bee hoped they didn't wake anyone. There was a tiny glow of sunlight beyond the buildings. It was a long ride on the local bus to reach the big bus station. They rode downtown without talking much. Only a few people were on the bus. An old man sat right behind the driver, snoring in his seat.

Sugar Bee was sleepier than she wanted to be, but she forced herself to stay awake. This was no morning to fall asleep. In twenty minutes they reached the station, a long narrow building with two rows of seats down the middle.

Clumps of people stood near the doors leading outside. Sugar Bee could see buses parked there, some backing out with a rumble and wheeze. They were much bigger than the city buses.

It was cold in the station as wind blew in through the open doors. Sugar Bee's coat was too short to keep her legs warm.

"Here, Sugar Bee, I have your ticket," her father said when he came back from the little window: "This part is for when you come back. Let Dr. Martin keep it for you."

"I will, Poppa," she answered.

Sugar Bee hadn't said much. She wanted to go, she had waited for this day. But now she had a sad feeling inside and it was growing bigger and bigger. Her mother smoothed her hair back. She hadn't even noticed it was loose.

"Mind yourself on the bus. Keep quiet and remember the driver knows you're going to Red Ridge. He'll watch out for you. And the Martins will meet you there. Remember to sit in the same seat and . . ." Her mother had many things to tell her at this last moment. But Sugar Bee had a hard time listening. She seemed to even have a hard time standing still or even breathing right.

A man's voice announced that a bus was leaving from Gate 4.

". . . for Beaver, New Castle, Mercer, Red Ridge . . ."

Mr. Harris got up quickly. "That's us. Come on, Momma, let's get our girl to Gate Four."

Sugar Bee took her mother's hand. That sadness got bigger and bigger. They stood in a line, surrounded by other people, most of them white men and women. No children at all, black or white.

Sugar Bee tugged hard at her mother's hand.

"I want to wait," she said suddenly.

"You want to wait?" her father asked in surprise. "Wait for what?"

Her mother knelt on the cement floor, her hand on Sugar Bee's face.

"Don't you want to go, Sugar Bee?"

Sugar Bee stood still, looking very worried.

"This is a fine chance for you, honey. This whole week with new people, new things. Very fine people. You'll like Red Ridge and the Martins. I know you will." Her mother's voice was low but firm.

Sugar Bee knew she had tears in her eyes when her mother hugged her. Together they followed her father to the bus. The seat behind the driver was empty and her father put the suitcase above it.

"I got you a few things to chew on while you ride," her father said, handing her a little sack. She held it so hard it squashed.

Her mother kissed her hard on both cheeks. "In a few hours you'll be there. Now you enjoy every-

thing, see everything. And learn a lot. Then you can tell us all about it when you come home."

Sugar Bee felt a lot of tears now. She wanted to go home, right now. Yet she wanted to ride the bus, to Red Ridge and the Martin family. How could anyone want different things at the same time? She felt miserable.

Her poppa stood in the door of the bus and winked. He left and her mother said cheerfully, "Now you be good, you hear?" They disappeared.

Sugar Bee got up on her knees. She could just see the top of her father's head. She couldn't see her mother at all.

The bus rumbled backwards and swung away. She was alone now, hunched in the seat.

The bus crossed one bridge after another. Pittsburgh had more bridges than she'd ever imagined. Rivers wandered here and there, cutting the city into pieces. Some bridges were modern, some old like castle bridges.

Sugar Bee kept her face to the sunny window. They passed factories and row upon row of apartments much like hers. But she knew they were already far from her street, her home. The sun warmed her and made her sleepy again. Hours slipped past as she dozed and then wakened again.

The driver called out many places where the bus stopped to let people off and take more on. But none were Red Ridge. They passed trees, fields, long rolling hills. Flocks of birds made the sky freckled. The bus turned away from the sun and rolled quickly down a smaller road. Houses and tall barns were set back from the road. They looked like play houses to Sugar Bee, neat squares with trees stuck around them like sticks in a sand-box.

Each field was like a brown box with wrinkles. Some fields were half green where the plows still worked. Sugar Bee saw that the "country" was mostly green, with splashes of color. Whole trees seemed made of pink, white or cherry red fluff.

The bus slowed. A little store and gas station sat side by side. As the bus stopped Sugar Bee leaned out into the aisle to see who would get off.

"Red Ridge," the bus driver called.

A lady entered the bus, looked around and came to Sugar Bee.

"Stephanie?" she asked. "I'm Mrs. Martin."

Sugar Bee tried to smile but couldn't manage it. The lady reached for her suitcase and took Sugar Bee's arm. "Shall we go home?"

Sugar Bee followed her off the bus where a man

was waiting. The bus door snapped shut and Sugar Bee was afraid again, like she had been when her mother had disappeared from sight.

A faded metal sign was swinging from a post, squeaking in the wind. RED RIDGE. The rumble of the bus faded and Sugar Bee heard another sound. A great flock of birds rose from a nearby field and Sugar Bee jumped at the sight and sound of them.

The man took Sugar Bee's suitcase and they all went to a dusty blue car parked under a spreading tree that looked quite dead. As he opened the car door, the man smiled at Sugar Bee.

"I'm Dr. Martin. Nice to have you with us, Stephanie."

Sugar Bee saw him smiling, she saw the car and the lady, but she didn't feel that any of this was real. Suddenly she was standing in a strange place between two people she had never seen before, and there was no way to go back, to go home.

She stared at the woman. Mrs. Martin was kind of round. Not fat, but heavier than her own mother. Her hair was reddish-gold and it fell to her shoulders in gentle waves. Her face was plain, no fancy makeup. But it was a pleasant face. Her skin was cream colored, and delicate.

Dr. Martin was quite tall and much thinner than her own poppa. He didn't have a thick lump at the waist like her poppa either. His hair thinned on top and he had a graying mustache. He wore glasses that glinted in the sun. His hand, holding her little suitcase, was slender but strong looking. His face was more sunburned than his wife's and he had bright blue eyes.

They were kind, friendly eyes and Sugar Bee tried to smile back at him. But it wasn't easy.

Sugar Bee sat between the Martins in the car, trying to tug her dress over her knobby knees.

"Did you have to get up very early?" Mrs. Martin asked.

Sugar Bee nodded, her hands folded in her lap. She hoped the lady didn't see the faded line on her dress.

"Did you enjoy the bus ride?" Dr. Martin glanced down at her.

She said yes very softly. She couldn't see much of the road as they drove, just trees so thick that their branches reached from both sides to touch in the middle. Their new leaves glowed in the sun like Christmas tree bulbs. As the car turned up a small lane, the branches brushed the top of the car and Sugar Bee pulled back against the seat.

She heard the barking of dogs, even over the

rattle and clank of the car. They stopped close to a tall white house which had pointed places with windows set in the steep slanted roof. As they got out two tiny dogs scampered up.

"Sit," Dr. Martin said.

The dogs settled on their haunches, tongues hanging. They almost looked like they were smiling. Sugar Bee heard other dogs barking, but she couldn't see them.

She stood still, gazing at the house. It rose high above her, framed against great trees that grew around it. A long porch crossed the front of it and carved white wood decorated the corners. Behind the railing were green wicker chairs, and a long-haired cat rubbed itself against a porch post.

Mrs. Martin called to a man sitting on a wooden crate at the side of the porch.

"Here we are, Sam, home with our special guest."

The man came toward them limping. He was very old. His eyes seemed out of shape as he peered at Sugar Bee through thick glasses. He held out his hand. His once white skin had yellowed with age and lumpy purple veins crisscrossed his many wrinkles. Sugar Bee held out her hand, not very far.

"What's your name, child?"

She almost said Sugar Bee. But she glanced at Mrs. Martin, the lady with the soft, rosy face.

She said in a clear voice, "My name is Stephanie Harris."

"That's a mighty fine name," the old man croaked. When he grinned she could see his teeth were missing here and there.

Mrs. Martin was standing on the steps, waiting for Sugar Bee to follow. She came up one stair at a time. They creaked like the stairs at home.

"This is our home, Stephanie. We hope you like it."

Right then Sugar Bee decided she would leave her nickname behind. She would be Stephanie now, and that would be wonderful.

6

A PATTERN of colored glass was set in the wooden front door. Stephanie, the all-the-time-Stephanie, could smell something cooking, the warm friendly smell of baking.

"Momma?"

A girl's voice called from the room ahead of them.

"Momma, is she here?"

Mrs. Martin took Stephanie by the hand and led her quickly through a hallway into a big room. The ceiling was higher than most rooms and the windows were tall and narrow. The rug on the floor was dark with a wide fringe. There was a piano in the far corner with thick round legs like the one in the school auditorium.

Stephanie saw a girl sitting on a couch near a window. The sunlight behind her made her hair look like it was on fire. The girl got up and came across the room, her hands out. Mrs. Martin stepped aside and gently moved Stephanie toward the girl.

"Hello. I'm Rosemary." The girl touched Stephanie on the shoulder and then took hold of her hand.

Stephanie was shy and she said "Hi" in almost a whisper.

"It seems like it took forever for you to get here," Rosemary said. "Momma says I'm too impatient."

Mrs. Martin laughed. "Well, Rosemary, why don't we take Stephanie up to your room and help her get settled?"

The girl went to the stairs holding tight to Stephanie's hand.

"Oh sure. Come on up."

They climbed the soft, carpeted stairs. The railing was smooth and shining.

"Did you like the bus ride?" the girl asked.

Stephanie said yes and looked at her. But the girl was turned away. They went through a door at the left of the top of the stairs. It led into a sunny room with two beds. Built under the window was a seat. White ruffled curtains made the room look fluffy all over. Stephanie took a quick breath. It was absolutely beautiful!

Mrs. Martin put Stephanie's suitcase on one bed. Rosemary sat on the other.

"This is usually my bed but if you would rather sleep here, you may."

Stephanie was staring out through the big windows. Green! There were trees everywhere, more green, glowing trees. She hadn't heard what Rosemary said to her. She didn't mean to stare, but everything inside and outside was so beautiful, so much like a dream. She stood nervously, not knowing what to say or where to move next. Mrs. Martin opened the suitcase.

"Let her get her things put away first. We'll use the bottom drawer. Rosemary has the others stuffed with all kinds of junk, don't you, Punkin?"

Rosemary rolled over on the bed. "Not junk, Momma. It's my . . . stuff."

Stephanie sat on the edge of the bed. It was soft and it smelled like starch. This was a marvelous room, with blue flowered wall paper, light blue spreads and even blue bows to hold back the curtains.

Mrs. Martin put Stephanie's things in the drawer. There wasn't much. She picked up the toothbrush and paste.

"I'll put these in the bathroom. Why don't you change into play clothes?"

She left. Rosemary stood up, her hand against the wall and went to the window seat. She opened it.

"This is where I keep my favorite things, Stephanie. If you have anything special with you, you can keep it in here too. Would you like to?" Rosemary was leaning over the open seat. She gestured to come and Stephanie walked to the window. She knelt down next to Rosemary.

"I guess so. But I didn't bring anything special," she said.

Then she remembered the ticket envelope in her coat pocket. She had forgotten to give it to Dr. Martin. She pulled it out.

"I have to give this to your father," she said, holding the envelope out toward Rosemary.

Rosemary put up her hand. She moved it slowly in front of her until her fingers touched the envelope.

"Momma will be right back. You can give it to her."

Stephanie kept staring at the other girl. She held the envelope very still. And then she knew something—something terrible.

Rosemary couldn't see the envelope in front of her. She couldn't see Stephanie kneeling next to her. Rosemary was blind.

Stephanie was frightened.

Mrs. Martin returned and came right to the window seat.

"Oh, so you've already shown off your special place, Rosemary. That's good. Do you have anything to keep in there, Stephanie?"

Stephanie was still on her knees, the envelope tight in her fist. She turned toward Mrs. Martin, her eyes wide.

"What's the matter? Did I startle you?" Mrs. Martin asked.

Stephanie bit her lip. She was fighting back the tears which were starting to fill her eyes and her hand was shaking.

"Oh," said Mrs. Martin, "is this your return ticket? I'll keep it in the desk downstairs." She took the envelope and went to the door.

"Rosemary, I'm going to show Stephanie the bathroom. Put on your jeans then you can both go out for a while."

Stephanie got up and followed Mrs. Martin, but she stopped for a moment to look back at Rosemary. The girl stood up and went to the dresser, one hand held just a tiny bit in front of her. Stephanie felt her tears running now.

Mrs. Martin was in the long cool bathroom with a stack of towels. "You can use these and whatever you need, just ask."

She turned toward Stephanie and saw the tears. Quickly she put her hand on Stephanie's cheek.

"Are you homesick? We want you to be happy this week."

Stephanie let her head droop. Mrs. Martin sat on the edge of the tub and lifted her head in her hand.

"What's the matter?" she whispered.

"Rosemary . . . Rosemary is . . ." Stephanie tried to say "blind" but she just couldn't use that word.

"Rosemary is blind," said Mrs. Martin. "Didn't you know?"

Stephanie shook her head and tears fell on her dress.

"No," she whispered.

"Oh . . ." Mrs. Martin sighed in a weary way.

She held on to Stephanie. "They should have told you. It would have been much easier. The school knew, but maybe your parents didn't know."

Stephanie sniffled. No, her parents couldn't have known, she thought. And now that she knew, she cried.

"Stephanie, listen carefully. Rosemary is blind, but that doesn't change her. She loves people and she wants to have you here this week. You'll have fun, I promise." Mrs. Martin spoke softly, without sadness. "Rosemary's a lot like you. Almost the same age. And she used to be able to see, just like you. But when she was seven she lost her sight and now she can't see at all. She just wants you to have a good time. There's so much you can do together. Lots of things. How about it? Think you two can have a good week?"

Stephanie wiped her eyes. "I'll try," she said, but she wasn't at all sure she could do it.

"That's good enough," Mrs. Martin said with a smile. She bent and smoothed Stephanie's hair, as her own mother always did. Then she pointed to Rosemary's room.

"Change your clothes and Rosemary will show you around."

Stephanie walked uncertainly back into the bedroom. Rosemary had put on her jeans.

"Ready to go? I want you to meet my friends," Rosemary said.

Stephanie changed quickly and they went downstairs. She could hardly believe it. Rosemary didn't walk down, she SKIPPED. And she kept right on skipping down the hall and onto the porch. Her fingers just skimmed the railing as she hopped to the driveway. A little picket fence ran around the house. Rosemary slid her fingertips from stick to stick as she talked to Stephanie.

"I bet you already met Yip and Yap."

The two tiny black dogs raced up and pranced around Rosemary on their hind legs. They were cute and Stephanie smiled her first smile since she had learned about Rosemary and her blindness.

"These two pests are Cairn Terriers. Daddy found them near the highway last year, abandoned. They were a mess but he fixed them up and no one ever came looking for them. So now they're ours."

A louder barking came from beyond the house. The gravel drive passed an open garage where the blue car was parked. Two cats were curled up on the hood. At the end of the drive was a wire fence. It was divided to form small pens. Each pen had a little shed at the back. Animals were inside. Rosemary walked straight across the driveway and crouched in front of the first pen.

"Get down here with me," Rosemary said. "The fawn won't come over unless you get near the ground."

They both crouched and Stephanie peered through the crisscrossed wire. In the far corner of the pen a small deer watched them with huge eyes. Stephanie could see it tremble. She didn't want to scare it, so she moved back a little.

"Don't go, Stephanie," Rosemary said, holding her sleeve. "She'll come over, just wait."

Rosemary made little tick-tick sounds with her tongue. The fawn fumbled a bit as it came to the fence and pushed its nose against the wire. Rosemary stuck her finger through and ran it up and down the fawn's throat. The tiny animal lifted its head higher.

"This is Snuffy. Listen to her when I pet her neck."

Stephanie heard it make a small blowing noise. It did sound snuffy. Rosemary moved to the next pen. She knew just how far to walk. A bony goat came crashing to the fence. Rosemary laughed and jiggled the wire.

"Take it easy, Grump!" she scolded.

The goat nibbled at the wire as if he would chew right through it. Stephanie giggled. No goat could chop that wire. Rosemary reached down and felt the ground. She pulled up a clump of grass as the goat climbed the fence with its front feet, clanking and rattling everything.

"What a beggar," she said as she threw the grass in the air. It fell near the goat and he snatched it, chewing like a machine.

"I call him Grump because he won't be friends unless you give him something to eat. That's really grumpy, don't you think?"

Stephanie nodded. Suddenly she remembered that wasn't enough. She would have to answer out loud. She said, "Yea, that's for sure."

In the third pen a calf lay next to a water crock. Its tail swished but it didn't get up.

"I call her Nellie. She's better now. When she came she had to be fed by hand but she still doesn't walk much." Rosemary said.

The back porch door opened and Mrs. Martin called to them.

"Dinner time, girls. Get washed."

Rosemary waved her hand. "We're coming, just a minute."

She took Stephanie's hand again. "Meet my other friend, then we'll eat."

In the last pen was the biggest dog Stephanie had ever seen. Maybe it wasn't even a dog, she thought.

"Bernie is a full-grown Saint Bernard. Isn't he a giant? I can hardly reach around his neck with all that hair. He's a mess to keep clean but I just love him. He's always thumping around."

The wire was pried apart in one place and Rosemary put her arm through as far as she could. The great dog curled his dripping tongue around the wire.

"Ack. You're drooling all over me, Bernie."

Rosemary was laughing as she stood up. She went to the very end of the fence quickly and surely. Without a pause she walked to the back porch.

"We can use the back porch sink to wash," she said and hurried inside. All the animals complained about being left behind, in the cold darkening evening, then settled down in their pens.

But Stephanie lingered. She stayed on the porch, listening. It grew still. What a strange feeling, to be able to listen for a single sound, to try to discover where one bird call came from. She turned her head quickly, trying to catch other, unknown sounds.

The wind had a sound. Quiet and real. Leaves blew along the dirt and even they had a sound. The screen door she held open had its own sound, a rusty creak. Even the wooden boards under her feet groaned as she rose up on her toes. It pleased her. In the city, even inside, sounds thundered at her day and night. Here, the evening quiet was a wonder.

But it was cold and she started to shiver. She took one last look and went inside.

7

STEPHANIE was glad the kitchen was warm.
A marvelous old stove in the corner was like
one Stephanie had seen in books. It was black
metal with fancy curved legs. A large pipe rose
from the back of it and disappeared into the ceiling. A real fire burned inside, not just rings of
flame like the stove at home. Pots steamed on its
broad top. She was not sure it was safe to get close,
but Mrs. Martin didn't seem bothered, as she
stirred round and round in one pot.

"Here, sit next to me," Rosemary said, patting a
chair with her hand. Stephanie noticed that she
held her chin up higher than most people.

Dr. Martin was reading a paper. It was folded
narrow, like Stephanie's father folded his, and Dr.

Martin stirred his coffee without looking at the cup, just like her father. Stephanie warmed up quickly and was suddenly very hungry.

The fifth chair gathered near the round table was empty and Dr. Martin went to the hallway. He called very loud.

"Dinnertime, Sam!"

Rosemary said, "Sometimes Sam falls asleep in his room before dinner and it takes a trumpet to wake him."

Mrs. Martin laughed. "Well, he's older, you know. And with a busybody like you around, he gets worn out quickly."

"I don't think I'm a busybody, do you Stephanie?"

Stephanie grinned. "No," she answered.

Dr. Martin sat down again, leaving his paper on the sink.

"Did you meet Rosemary's friends yet?" he asked Stephanie.

Rosemary answered for her. "I took her around the pens, Daddy. Grump almost wrecked the fence trying to meet her. He's all well now, isn't he?"

"Almost, honey. Another few days and he can go home."

The porch door slammed. Sam came in, bundled in a jacket and scarf.

"Rain tonight," he announced in a raspy voice.

"The paper says clear all weekend," Dr. Martin answered.

"Hrummp! Newspapers don't know nothin'. How's a danged reporter going to tell the weather with his nose stuck in a desk? Gotta walk and study the sky, feel the wind, sniff how it blows. Then a body can tell about weather."

"And the wind says rain?" Mrs. Martin asked, filling his bowl.

"Sure do," Sam muttered as he took a big slab of cornbread and a great glob of butter. "Might even thunder some. Is this little city lady 'fraid of thunder?" He squinted at Stephanie.

"Stephanie isn't afraid of anything, are you, Stephanie?" Rosemary asked quickly.

Stephanie still had her hands in her lap. She hadn't eaten anything because she didn't want to reach. She was going to answer the question but Rosemary chattered on.

"Grump didn't scare her and he can even scare BOYS. May I have the honey, please, Stephanie?"

Stephanie picked up the little jar and held it

toward Rosemary. She touched it to her fingers. Rosemary took it and didn't even drip on the tablecloth.

Mrs. Martin filled each bowl with bubbling ham and beans and passed a platter of hot cornbread.

"That there calf kicked over its feed again, Doc. Ain't ailin' like it was," Sam said, dunking a tea bag and sloshing the table.

"She's going home tomorrow. Silver Dairy has a lamb that needs care. We'll use the calf pen for it," Dr. Martin said, taking more cornbread and butter.

Stephanie wondered about it when old Sam said "Doc." She knew Rosemary's father was a doctor even though he didn't dress like one.

"Daddy, is it a new lamb that's coming, a really little one?"

"It's a little one, Rosemary, and it'll need hand feeding. But I know you won't have time for any of that," he said, winking at Stephanie.

"Rosemary's father is teasing," Mrs. Martin said. "This girl of ours would hand feed every animal in the county if she had a chance. She feeds animals almost as well as their mothers do."

"Momma, this time Stephanie can do it." Rosemary sounded pleased with her own idea. "It's fun, Stephanie. We'll take turns. Lambs are the best. They feel fluffed up and kinky, and they make a little, bitty sound, like this. Bahaaaaa, bahaaaaaa."

Everyone at the table laughed. Rosemary *did* sound like some kind of animal but not much like a lamb. They had all finished their beans and Mrs. Martin got up.

"These are our own plums, dear," she told Stephanie as she served plump purple fruit from a glass jar. "They grow in the orchard beyond the garage."

"They're really good. I help can them. Does your mother can fruits and things?" Rosemary asked.

Stephanie didn't know about such things. They had fruit at home but it didn't come in jars like that. It came from cans.

"No, I don't think so," she answered Rosemary.

"Momma cans lots of fruit and vegetables, too. In the summer Sam grows the biggest tomatoes you ever ate in the garden. Do you have a garden in your yard?"

Stephanie shook her head, she didn't have a

garden. She didn't have a yard. Mrs. Martin saw her shaking her head and she tickled Rosemary under the chin.

"Now, silly little country girl. Most apartments don't have yards and Stephanie lives in an apartment. How could she have a garden?"

"Oh, that's right. But anyhow you'll like plums. And when we're done we can play the piano," Rosemary hurried on.

"Slow down," her mother said. "You have all evening. First, dishes, you know."

Rosemary made a face. "Ugh. Dishes. Do you have to do dishes Stephanie?"

Stephanie said, "Yes. I do them every night."

"All of them?"

"No, just dry. Sometimes I wash too."

"I only have to dry," Rosemary said, taking a dish towel from a rack on the wall. Stephanie took one too.

Mrs. Martin washed and stacked the dishes in the rack. Rosemary picked up the dishes carefully and wiped both sides, running her finger around to be sure each was dry. Working together they were done in no time.

"Want me to play you something on the piano?" Rosemary asked as they went to the front room.

She pulled out the bench and it wobbled a bit because the leg was cracked at the bottom.

"I know some music but my teacher moved. Now I have to wait until summer before I can take more lessons."

Stephanie didn't understand that. How could anyone play the piano if they couldn't see it? But she didn't ask Rosemary such a question.

"I didn't mean to take up the whole bench," Rosemary said, moving over a little. "But I have to be in the middle so I know which keys are in front of me."

She spread her fingers on the keys and made a chord. Her fingers ran up and down the keys and it was beautiful. Stephanie didn't know anything about playing a piano. She couldn't even make a chord with three fingers. The only piano she had touched was at school. And the janitor only unlocked it when a teacher was there to lift the keyboard cover and play.

"Can you play?" Rosemary asked as she made several high chords.

"No. My friend Mary Lou can but not me."

"Well then, I can teach you something."

They sat there for a long time, Rosemary carefully shaping Stephanie's hand over the keys.

Stephanie tried to keep her fingers apart but it wasn't easy. But after several tries she could get them down where they belonged and sound a chord. It was really quite pretty.

Dr. Martin had joined them and sat smoking his pipe. The smoke drifted in under the lamp shade and curled like ribbons. The phone rang in the hall. Stephanie could hear Mrs. Martin answer it.

"Yes, Dr. Martin is home, just a minute."

She came in to Dr. Martin. "Dear, it's Judd Carver. The mare isn't doing too well on her own."

Rosemary slid off the piano bench and went into the hall while her father answered the call.

"No. Don't try anything until I get there." He looked serious.

He hung up and Mrs. Martin already had his coat ready. He took the car keys from the hall table. "This might take some time."

He kissed Rosemary. "What'll we name the foal, honey?"

"Call it . . . let's see. Call it Champion Call, Daddy."

"Champion Call, huh? Well, I'll tell Judd. He's your buddy and he just might like that name."

They all went to the back door with him. Mrs. Martin held it open. It was dark and blustery and a few drops of rain blew in. Sam was right. Rain was on the way. Dr. Martin hurried toward the garage as they shut the door.

Somewhere in the house there was a gong-gong. Stephanie knew it was a clock, maybe like the one in the Thrift Shop, pretty but usually wrong. Mrs. Martin had counted the gongs.

"Nine. Time for bed, girls. You can talk all night if you want to, but head for bed."

Rosemary put the lid down on the piano and pushed the bench back in place. Stephanie watched her move around the room. She even stopped to touch the newspapers on the low table. She straightened them. And she hummed one little tune she had played on the piano.

Together they went upstairs, not in a hurry like they had done in the afternoon. They were both tired and went up one stair at a time. Stephanie noticed the carpet on the stairs was worn out in the middle. The rug was old and ragged. That surprised Stephanie. She had thought it was quite new and beautiful when she first came in.

Rosemary flopped on her bed. "Wouldn't it be great if Judd did name the foal 'Champion'?" She propped her chin on her hands. "Oh, but you don't know about Judd Carver, do you?"

"Nope," Stephanie answered.

"Judd raises horses. He's really rich, I guess. Anyhow he thinks he knows everything in the whole world about horses. But whenever there's trouble he runs to the phone to call Daddy. Daddy knows more about horses than Judd or anybody." She rolled over again.

"Does your father fix horses, too?" Stephanie asked softly.

"Sure. He's great with horses. And even a messy goat like Grump."

"But your father's a doctor," Stephanie said, puzzled.

"I know. He's the best doctor in Red Ridge. He even goes into Beaver sometimes to treat race horses."

"But how come he fixes horses? Doesn't he fix people?"

Rosemary sat straight up on her bed. Then she rolled over and over, laughing.

"He's not a people doctor! Oh, Stephanie," she laughed. "He's a veterinarian. An animal doctor."

She bounced so hard on the bed that it shook

two books off the shelf against the wall. Mrs. Martin stuck her head in the door.

"What's going on in here, a circus?"

"Oh, Momma! Stephanie asked me the funniest question. She asked if Daddy fixed PEOPLE!" Rosemary was almost out of breath from laughing.

Stephanie sat on the other bed, feeling hurt. She hadn't meant to ask a stupid question.

Mrs. Martin grabbed Rosemary's foot.

"Settle down, my red-headed clown. You're not being a good hostess. You're not even being polite. Stephanie didn't understand what your father does. There are a lot of different kinds of doctors. You'll make her feel bad if you keep this up."

Rosemary scooted off the bed and stood close to Stephanie.

"I wasn't laughing at you. Honest. I just thought it was funny, about Daddy fixing people. I won't laugh anymore. All right?"

"O.K.," Stephanie said, but she didn't feel o.k. She had a lump in her throat and her insides were tight. Mrs. Martin took her hand.

"Now, Rosemary, just sit there and behave. Stephanie is going to take a bath and she'll sleep better."

Stephanie stood by while Mrs. Martin got things

ready for her. She set out large towels and wash cloths, a rose-shaped bar of scented soap and a bottle of foaming bath oil. It was quite a preparation. The tub was extra long and edged with light green tile that reached half way up the wall. Mrs. Martin turned on the electric wall heater.

"If you need anything else, just pound on the wall. Rosemary will come."

Stephanie was alone in the immaculate bathroom. Water gushed from the faucet, filling the tub. She let it swirl around her as she poured the bath oil into the water. It was like pretending, only this was real. At home there was a bathroom. One. Shared by every family on their floor. One dingy, smelly room that all those people used because they had to.

And here she was, alone in this warm, shiny place with fragrant soap and steaming hot water to make her feel better. But it didn't. It made her feel guilty. All of this for her? She felt selfish and not even the sweet smell of the bath oil could change it. She was finished quickly.

She and Rosemary were in bed by nine-thirty, all lights turned out. Rain hit the windows like many curious fingers. Thunder rumbled far away. Rosemary talked softly about animals but Stephanie didn't really listen. Her mind was not in that blue and white room. It was many miles away. She thought about her mother and father. They would be alone, too. She wondered if the storm reached all the way to Pittsburgh.

She wanted to be home. On the very first night of her special week she was afraid. Just like Mary Lou had warned. Now the night storm seemed to be warning her too. A gust of wind rattled the windows. Stephanie shuddered to think what Maudie would have told her, if the old black witch had read her hand. What would Maudie have seen ahead for one young black girl all by herself in such a different place?

Stephanie remembered Gloria, her beautiful face twisted so strangely when she talked about "charity." But this was her trip, she had earned it, like her mother said. And she had waited, marking off each day on her calendar. Now it wasn't at all what she had dreamed. If Miss Bloom had just picked someone else, anyone . . .

"Stephanie, are you sleeping?" Rosemary whispered.

"No."

"You know, sometimes kittens are born during storms. There's one litter already, born four weeks ago. Another female is ready to have hers any time, and I'll bet she'll have them tonight. Daddy'll give you one of the older kittens to keep." She paused. "But gosh, maybe you already have a cat or something."

"No," Stephanie answered. She didn't want to talk, to risk saying something foolish again.

"Nothing? Not even a dog?"

"No, I don't," she mumbled.

She had wanted a kitten once, but sooner or later the dogs and cats in her neighborhood were killed or crippled by cars and trucks. If she had a kitten she'd just worry about it all the time.

"Would your mother say o.k. about a kitten?" Rosemary asked.

Stephanie didn't know what her mother would say. So she lied. Just a little lie, but it was still a lie.

"No, she doesn't like cats."

Rosemary fluffed up her pillow. "That's too bad. But if your momma says no, I guess it's no."

Stephanie huddled in the bed. Now she had blamed her mother for something that wasn't true. It was all wrong. She didn't belong here, in a house full of white people with their pretty stuff and animals all over.

"Tomorrow will you tell me about the city?" Rosemary had excitement in her voice.

Stephanie said nothing.

"It's really different from out here in the country, isn't it?"

Stephanie lay very still. Yes, it was different. It was big and noisy and ugly and gray. But it was where she belonged. Not here.

"Will you tell me, huh?"

"Sure," Stephanie whispered. But there were tears on her cheeks.

8

SUN SPLASHED all over the bedroom and Stephanie woke up blinking. A marvelous smell hung in the air. Rosemary was up, dressing. Stephanie watched her for a few moments. It isn't right to lie here staring at someone who can't see, she thought. She climbed out of the spring bed.

Rosemary turned. "Are you awake?" She sounded chipper and fresh.

"Yes," Stephanie answered, still squinting in the brightness.

"I smell cinnamon rolls and bacon. Let's go eat," Rosemary said. Stephanie got into her jeans and blouse in a hurry.

Dr. and Mrs. Martin were waiting for them in the kitchen. Stephanie smiled a little when they asked her how she slept. The smell of food and a good sleep had done something special—they'd made her feel almost happy.

Rosemary had a mouthful of roll when she remembered the horse.

"Daddy, did the foal come? What happened?"

Dr. Martin was in the middle of a yawn.

"Sure did. About midnight. Took her time, too."

"What did Judd call the foal? Did he like Champion?"

"Nope. He picked out 'Destiny Doll.' How do you like that?"

"That's a beautiful name," Stephanie said quietly.

"Do you like it?" Rosemary asked in surprise.

Stephanie frowned. Had she said the wrong thing again?

"So do I, Stephanie," Mrs. Martin said as she took off her apron. "Now we'd better all hustle or we'll be late for church."

"Stephanie, you can come with us or stay with Sam till we come back. It's up to you," Dr. Martin said.

She paused. "I guess I'll come," she said.

The girls went upstairs to change into dresses.

Rosemary brushed her long straight red hair. Stephanie fretted with hers. Mrs. Martin followed them into the bedroom and within a few moments had Stephanie's hair smoothed neatly and pulled loosely back into a rubber band.

"Let me see your dress," Rosemary said.

Stephanie stood still. She didn't know what Rosemary meant. Rosemary came closer and put her fingers on the dress. She touched the collar, the buttons and the belt.

"What color is it?"

"Sort of white with daisies on it," Stephanie murmured.

"It's nice. Do you like mine?"

Rosemary wore a blue jumper with white blouse. At the bottom of the jumper was a faded line, just like the one on Stephanie's dress.

"It's real pretty," Stephanie said.

The drive to church was like wandering through a picture book. Farms nestled among the endless trees. There were many little bridges which made a hollow rump-a-rump when the blue car crossed over them.

A slender steepled white church stood atop a hill. Cars were gathered beneath it. Children chased each other while grownups waved to each other and talked. Stephanie had seen such churches on Christmas cards. There was always snow and ladies in long dresses and fluffy hats. Now the ground was chocolate brown patched with green. Bare trees were pencil sketched against the clouding sky.

In the church they sang and knelt for prayers after the sermon. It was cold inside. Stephanie spent most of the time looking at the windows. Morning sunlight changed into rainbow hues, coloring the women's hats and making patterns on the floor. It was another beautiful place. Her Sunday school in the city was in the basement of the rambling church and it always smelled moldy and dank. There they had large water pipes overhead, instead of graceful wooden beams.

After the service the Martins met friends outside. Rosemary kept saying, "This is my friend, Stephanie." Some women asked her how she was but none of the children spoke to her. Some children leaned out of the windows of their family cars and watched her. She knew they stared.

It started to rain. Dr. Martin called to them to hurry and get into the car. Stephanie kept her face against the window as they drove back to the farm. Everything was worth seeing, worth remembering so she could tell her mother, as she had promised.

Sunday was a quiet day. Only necessary work was done. The animals were fed, the house straightened. Mrs. Martin put a large beef roast in the oven for the evening meal and made muffin batter.

"Can we have a picnic lunch?" Rosemary asked as her mother spooned the yellow batter into the pan.

"That's a fine idea." Her mother nodded. "But it's soaking wet outside. The only dry place is in the garage and who wants to eat in a garage?"

"Oh phooey!" Rosemary said, thumping her foot against the cupboard.

"Can we pretend? You know, take some stuff up to my room and pretend we're on a picnic?" She tugged at her mother's apron, teasing.

"What stuff? You can't spoil your appetite for dinner, but I guess you could take a little something to snack on if you really want." Her mother smiled.

"We do! Don't we, Stephanie?" Rosemary was dragging her to the pantry, a large walk-in cupboard where Mrs. Martin stored her canned foods, spices, vegetables and other good things. It had the most interesting aroma. Stephanie sniffed. Ummm, good.

They found a bowl and filled it with two apples,

some potato chips and several cookies apiece. They poured themselves two large glasses of milk. Then, very carefully, they made their way upstairs. Rosemary told Stephanie where to find a blanket to spread on the floor next to the window seat. Their picnic was ready.

"There won't be any ants," Rosemary said, laughing as she munched her apple. She had pulled a huge book onto the floor and as she opened the pages, Stephanie stared at it. There were no words. None at all.

"This is Braille," Rosemary explained. "I read bumps with my fingers like I used to read words. It took a long time to learn how, but I'm quite fast now. Want to try?"

Stephanie shook her head no but Rosemary had already reached out and placed her hand on the page. It *was* bumpy, just a mass of bumps that didn't mean a thing to Stephanie.

"You just use the tips of your fingers. It's a pattern and spells things out. This one's about a horse, *Black Beauty*. The Braille Institute has a lot of books they send around. I read a lot and I listen, too."

Rosemary moved to a black box on her bedside table. It was a tape recorder. Stephanie had seen one in a store near the apartment. And a young

man in their apartment had a little one that he set on the front window sill during the summer so the kids could listen. Rosemary pushed several buttons and the tape began to revolve slowly. A woman's voice was reading, telling a story with a lot of feeling, almost like a play.

"That's Dorothy. She's a regular reader and I get a lot of the books she tapes."

Stephanie was as puzzled by this as she was by the Braille book. The woman who was reading on the recorder coughed and then said, "Sorry about that," just like she was sitting in the room with them.

Rosemary laughed. "She's funny. Sometimes she thinks of a joke and just stops the story to tell it. You never know just what she's going to say. I like her best of all the readers."

"Readers?" Stephanie had a question in her voice.

"Oh, there I go again. I don't explain things. Momma is nagging me about that a lot. Readers are people who volunteer to read whole books onto recording tape. Then they send them around to kids like me and we listen. We just got this tape recorder last Christmas. And I almost wore it out the first week."

Rosemary shut it off and put her big Braille book away.

"Last night you promised to tell me about the city. But first . . ." She seemed to be trying to find the words she wanted. "I sure hope you like it here. I'm awfully glad your folks let you come. Momma was worried that you wouldn't be happy."

Stephanie thought about the night before. She hadn't been happy, then. And she would have left, if she could have. But today was different.

"I guess we should have a room for you for your own, so you wouldn't have to share mine. I hope you don't mind. Do you have to share your bedroom with your sister or anybody?"

Stephanie bit her lip. She had no bedroom, just her little nook. She didn't want to tell Rosemary that.

"I don't have a sister," she said simply.

"Oh. Just you and your folks?"

"Yea."

"Same here. I don't have anybody else either. Except the animals and they come and go a lot."

Rosemary fumbled around for the potato chips. Stephanie pushed the bowl closer to her.

"Do you like school?" Rosemary asked.

"Sometimes."

"What do you like best?"

Stephanie shrugged. Some days it was English and Miss Bloom; some days it was singing, if Tommy Blue kept quiet.

"I like history best," Rosemary said, answering her own question. "Stories about knights and queens, with real castles. That's what I like best." She propped her feet on her bed.

"Do you live close to school?"

"About six blocks."

"Do you ride a bike?"

Stephanie frowned. The few bikes on her block were either stolen or busted up by kids who didn't like each other.

"No, I walk," she answered.

"Do you have parties in class when someone has a birthday? We do and the teacher lets us bring our favorite record."

Stephanie had never heard of such a thing. To her, school meant a lot of kids jammed in ugly rooms trying to keep their feet warm. Who would have a party at school? Not at her school. She wondered what Miss Bloom would say if someone asked for a party. Probably send him right into Mr. Goodstead's office.

"We don't do that. The teacher wouldn't like

it," she said in a dull way. She didn't want to talk about school, her school, about the city. It was ugly like a lot of things. She tried to change the talk to other places.

"It sure is pretty out here. Trees grow all over like a park."

Rosemary nodded. "I guess it is sort of like a park. Do you live near one?"

"No. The bus goes to Schenley Park, but I don't go there."

"Can't your father take you or your mother?"

"They work. And the park isn't open at night."

"Does your mother work, too?" Rosemary sounded surprised.

"Yes." Stephanie didn't see why that should surprise anyone.

"You mean at the church or something?"

"No. She works at Bimbos."

Rosemary giggled. "What's Bimbos?"

"It's where you eat," Stephanie yawned. It was a sleepy day.

"Oh, a restaurant. Do they have candles and flowers on the tables? Daddy took us to a fancy place near Beaver when I was little. It had fat red candles on round tables and pots of flowers. I was real little but I remember those candles."

Stephanie sat quietly. There sure weren't any

candles at Bimbos. Just a long counter and two booths against the greasy walls. There was a fly specked picture of a white girl drinking soda but no roses.

"They don't use candles there," Stephanie said under her breath.

It seemed like every time Rosemary talked, it was about things *she* didn't have or things she had never seen, fancy things. Stephanie was getting that lonely feeling again.

"Hey, I know!" Rosemary leaned toward her. "Let's ask Momma to use her candles for dinner tonight. Want to?"

Stephanie could tell Rosemary was pleased by her own idea. So she answered the way she should answer, even though she didn't really mean it.

"O.K. I guess so. That would be nice."

It would be nice, Stephanie thought to herself, to go to a place where there were flowers and candles on little tables and eat fancy food. That's what she would do if she could. She'd take her mother's hand and they'd walk right in. A man in a funny tie would bring them ice cream and noodle soup. And her mother would just sit and look pretty.

Dinner was special that evening. Mrs. Martin had reached up in the hall closet and brought out two glass candlesticks. She found two yellow candles wrapped in tissue, and she let Stephanie arrange them. She even took time to show Stephanie how to fold the paper napkins in peaks like she'd seen it done in magazines. The roast was crusty brown and the muffins light. The family ended the day together. Stephanie felt that now she really was welcome. The whole week lay ahead. It was going to be a good week.

9

MONDAY was for discovering.

The sun warmed everything, trying to act like summer. Breakfast was eaten in a hurry. Too much was waiting outside to waste time on eating.

"The lamb comes today," Rosemary said as they sauntered past the pens. "Once we had a black lamb here. The others shoved it around and it couldn't get food. It was sort of stunted."

Stephanie glanced at her fingers, bumping along the wire. They were very dark next to Rosemary's pale skin.

"The sun feels warm, doesn't it? Now, what do you want to do?" Rosemary asked, letting her shoe make streaks in the dirt.

"I don't know? What do you think?" Stephanie shrugged.

"O.K. I'll settle it. We'll go to the stream first. It's best," Rosemary said, kicking up a big clump of mud.

Stephanie looked anxiously at the back porch. Should Mrs. Martin know that they were going somewhere? Should they ask permission?

"Follow me," Rosemary said, crossing the driveway. She was going toward the first row of trees beyond the garage. Stephanie hesitated. Should she follow, or call Mrs. Martin?

Rosemary paused less than a foot away from the first tree. Stephanie watched her. How did she know when to stop? What made her stop right in front of it without bumping into it?

"Hurry up. I know you're not following me," Rosemary called.

Stephanie came and stood next to her.

"Are you worried about me?"

"Sort of," Stephanie admitted.

"I know where I am. I just raise my voice and listen."

"Listen?" Stephanie asked. That didn't make sense.

"The sound of my voice bounces off things—

trees, walls. So I know when I'm close to something and I stop. There's a rope around this tree. Daddy strung it and I use it to go where I want."

Rosemary stepped to her right and found the rope, just as she said she could. She let her hand slide back and forth. The rope led from one tree to the next. She moved freely, hitting nothing. Stephanie stayed beside her, more surprised all the time.

Stephanie took a deep breath. The country morning air tingled her nose. It almost had a soapy smell, delicate. No yellow haze spoiled the sunlight. No grayness blanketed the distant trees and hills.

"These are the plum trees. The blossoms are late but some are out." Rosemary shook a branch and petals floated down and lay on her red hair. They drifted between Stephanie's open fingers, like giant snowflakes.

They were going downhill and Rosemary held on to the rope. Stephanie could hear water splashing, moving somewhere. Through a bush she saw a bright, glittering streak at the bottom of the hill.

"Shusssh," Rosemary whispered. She held her head high. "Sometimes I can hear animals at the stream. If I'm very quiet they don't run away. Try to be quiet."

Stephanie bent lower to the ground, watching so her feet wouldn't crunch on leaves or sticks. Rosemary, guided by the rope, put one foot slowly in front of the other. She didn't make a sound. Stephanie stopped. Two ground squirrels were erect on a rock just in front of them.

The stream, trees and rocks, stacked atop each other, looked familiar to Stephanie, but she hadn't been here before. Then she remembered that it looked like a picture Miss Bloom showed the class once.

"Squirrels," Rosemary said softly.

How did she know they were there?

"Hear them chitter?"

In a wink the squirrels scurried off the rock and vanished into a hole.

"Now we can sit on the rock. Those little guys won't share it. They just take off." Rosemary laughed.

"They went in a hole," Stephanie said, still whispering.

"Sometimes they climb a tree," Rosemary said without whispering. "They sure are fast. I can tell how long it takes them to get up a tree."

She felt for the rock then let go of the rope and sat down. The rock was warm in the sun and had little scooped out places just right for sitting.

"Sometimes I put my feet in the water. But we'd better not today. It's still like ice water, this early in the spring."

Stephanie had been thinking about doing just that. Instead she dipped her hand in the water. Brrrr. It was icy.

"Do you come down here every day?" Stephanie asked.

"Usually, if there's no school. But boy, that takes up a lot of days. I like school, but I'd rather be down here."

Stephanie looked down, fascinated by the foamy water that swirled at the base of the rocks. She thought of the gutters along the streets at home. Water ran there, too, when it rained. But it was full of trash and even old shoes. Here the water was clear and looked clean enough to drink.

"Can you drink this?" she asked.

"Daddy says it's not a good idea 'cause it isn't pure like it used to be. I do drink it sometimes. That's not being bad, do you think?"

"Do you get sick when you do it?" Stephanie was curious.

"No, but I don't want to make him mad. You can take a drink if you want to."

Stephanie paused, but only for a moment. She knelt on the squishy moss and it soaked her pants knees. The water jumped in spurts and she leaned close. It splashed and when she did get a mouthful it was so cold it hurt her teeth. But it was delicious.

"That's good," she said, wiping her chin.

Rosemary laughed. "Don't fall in. I did a couple of times and Momma gave me the dickens." As she spoke, Rosemary swung around and felt for her rope.

"Let's go back to the pens. I'll bet the lamb is here by now."

They hurried uphill and Stephanie forgot to worry about Rosemary. There was no need. She could move as fast as she wished.

In the distance Stephanie saw a truck parked in the Martin driveway.

"There's a yellow truck," she said, panting a little.

"Does it say 'Silver Dairy' on it?"

"I think so," Stephanie said, straining to see.

Rosemary was already trotting ahead toward the pens. Two men stood near the rear of the truck, lifting a box with high wooden sides. Dr. Martin was cleaning out an empty pen. Rosemary made her way to the truck and ran her hand along the side until she was next to the box.

"Hi, Red," one of the men said with a toothy grin. In his arms was a sick-looking lamb. Stephanie was surprised that it was so small. He let the lamb down into the pen. It flopped on its knees then got up and tried to run out the pen door. Dr. Martin caught it and knelt to examine it.

"We'll keep her a few days just in case this trouble's contagious," he said. He stood up and brushed his knees.

They left the pen and after a few parting words the men got in their truck.

"So long, Red. Take care of that lamb, it's going to need it."

Rosemary called back to the man. "I'll try. And I'm not Red!"

She smiled when she said it, so Stephanie knew the nickname didn't make her mad. But nicknames could be awful. She ought to know.

Rosemary headed for the pen right away. She felt for the latch then waited. "Stephanie, want to come in with me? The poor thing will be too scared to eat if we don't help it."

Stephanie didn't want to go in there but Rosemary was waiting.

"O.K.," she said, and she followed Rosemary.

Rosemary sat, her legs folded under her. Stephanie crouched beside her, watching the lamb huddled in a corner. Rosemary made little tick-tick sounds again. The animal ignored both of them, bumping against the wire and wobbling around. It seemed like they waited a very long time. Stephanie wanted to leave but she could tell Rosemary didn't.

Little by little the lamb came closer, finally sagging to the ground. Rosemary turned her head a bit and could tell just where the lamb was lying by the sound of it. She got on her knees and moved forward a tiny bit, then a tiny bit more. The lamb stayed quietly in front of her. When she reached it, her fingers stroked its side gently and she began to talk to it.

"What's the matter, little one? Are you sick and all by yourself?" Her voice was soft and soothing. She touched its head, its thin legs and funny ears. "Pretty baby, don't shiver. I love you."

Stephanie was on the other side of the lamb. She could see it shiver and she could see other things too.

"You're beautiful, baby. We'll make you well," Rosemary said over and over as she slipped her arm around its neck. "Isn't it sweet, Stephanie? Such a tiny thing."

But Stephanie shook her head. It wasn't a beautiful lamb. It was bony and had runny eyes. Its fleece was almost gone in many spots. Something had injured it and there were patches of blood on its back. One part of its front leg was swollen and it was crusted with mud under its belly.

Stephanie could only think of one word—ugly. The lamb Rosemary kept calling "beautiful" was sick and ugly.

"Pick a name for it, Stephanie. I always give names to animals, even if they only stay for a day or two. You pick a name this time."

Stephanie frowned at the lamb. How could she give that thing a name? Rosemary tipped her head up as she gently cradled the lamb.

"I don't know any names," Stephanie said uneasily.

"It doesn't have to be a fancy name. Just a good name for a pretty little lamb," Rosemary said with a smile. The lamb struggled to get away but Rosemary held it. Staring at the dirty, kinky fur, Stephanie just couldn't think up a name. She crossed her fingers.

"Why not call it Beautiful, like you first did?" Stephanie said heavily. She could almost taste the little lie in her mouth.

"Should I, really?" Rosemary asked, and Stephanie could tell the name pleased her.

"Sure," Stephanie lied.

"There, now you have a name. My Beautiful," Rosemary said, hugging the bedraggled lamb. Just then Sam came in the pen with a feeding bottle. But as much as Rosemary coaxed, the lamb wouldn't suck on it. It was too sick to even try.

Darkness seemed to catch up with them quickly that day as they helped Sam change the water in the chicken coops. The wind grew harsh and they were glad to go into the house.

Dr. Martin had logs burning in the stone-faced fireplace. Stephanie stood very close but she found out quickly that a real fire had to be enjoyed from a distance. She and Rosemary sprawled on the dark rug. Yip and Yap had sneaked in the kitchen door and Mrs. Martin let them lie in the front room next to the couch. Yip kept crawling inch by inch until he was almost in Rosemary's lap. His tail swept back and forth as if he had a motor running it.

"I'm going to be a veterinarian too, huh, Daddy?" Rosemary piped up when everything had grown quiet. Dr. Martin dozed in his chair and didn't hear her.

"Well, I am," Rosemary told Stephanie. "Anyone can do it, if they study. I really want to. Are you going to college?" She sounded very grown-up to Stephanie.

Stephanie had never thought about college. Even high school was still a long way away.

"I don't think so," she mumbled, as she stared steadily at the fire.

"Oh, sure you will," Rosemary said in that perky, final voice of hers. The way she spoke seemed to settle matters with no doubts.

"Daddy went to college and so did Momma. But she quit. Daddy has his diploma in a frame. Momma says I can frame mine too when I get it."

The fire crackled and sizzled, a good sound. Stephanie was remembering Sydney, a boy from her block who went away to college. But he wrote his mother a letter and told her he left college to be a bricklayer. His mother had cried for days. It seemed a lot of fuss just for that.

"Did your daddy go to college, Stephanie?" Rosemary asked the question twice because Stephanie was deep in her thoughts and didn't hear.

"Unhuh—I mean, no," she answered.

"What does he do?" Rosemary kept on.

"My poppa? He drives a truck." She wished she had the picture on the calendar with her. "A big truck!" she added.

"Do you get to ride in it?" Rosemary was interested.

Stephanie wanted to say yes, to pretend that she rode anywhere she wanted in that great truck, but it wasn't true.

"It's full of pipes and stuff. I can't ride in it. But my poppa wears a jacket with the company name on it. I have a picture of him with his truck." She glanced at Rosemary. A picture wouldn't help the soft-faced girl beside her.

Mrs. Martin poked the fire and it spattered and popped. Rosemary knew her mother was nearby.

"Momma, Stephanie should go to college, shouldn't she?"

Mrs. Martin smiled. "College is wonderful, if you want it enough to work for it. What would you want to be, Stephanie?"

Stephanie had no answer ready for such a question. There were times when she would pretend to do fancy, special things that she really couldn't do. Like dancing. She liked to pretend that she could dance on a stage, in a ruffled costume with the lights on her. That was just one of her daydreams. So she used it.

"A dancer," she answered.

"That's fine. It takes a lot of study."

Mrs. Martin believed her!

"Yes, I guess so." Stephanie squirmed. She was stuck with her little pretending.

"Do they teach dancing in college?" Rosemary asked.

"Oh, yes. There are many fine schools that teach the arts, my dear," Mrs. Martin said lightly.

"Then you ought to go there, Stephanie. Then you could frame your diploma, like me."

Stephanie didn't answer. College was a dream. School was hard. There wouldn't be any room for a skinny black girl from Pittsburgh in a dancing school. Not for her. Her poppa didn't have a diploma—just a picture of a truck. Why waste time talking about dreams and wishes? She frowned at the fire embers.

"Bedtime, sleepyheads," Mrs. Martin said, nudging Rosemary's long legs with her foot.

As they went through the hall Mrs. Martin paused. Above the old clock was a frame that held a yellowing paper. She took it off the wall and handed it to Stephanie.

"It took Dr. Martin a long time to get this. It was hard for all of us and a couple of times he had to quit college, get a job and then go back. But he kept at it because he loved to work with animals and he wanted to do it right." She lifted Stephanie's face in her hand.

"If you dream about dancing, you have to try, too. If you really want it, you will be a fine dancer. But it takes work. Anything good takes work.

"Up to bed and wash," she said quickly. She disappeared into the kitchen.

Rosemary had gone to the front door. She held it open for a few moments and it chilled them both. They could hear a weak bleating. The sick lamb was alone in the dark pen.

"Good night, my Beautiful. Don't be afraid. Daddy will make you better," Rosemary said. Of course the lamb heard nothing, but Stephanie did. She looked back at the frame hung above the clock. If he had studied and worked so hard for that paper, then Dr. Martin surely must be able to fix the lamb. Poor, ugly thing. Why did they all care about it? She watched Rosemary climbing the stairs. Maybe, being ugly didn't matter if someone cared about you, loved you, like Rosemary loved her "Beautiful."

10

IN THE MORNING Rosemary fed the lamb with a bottle. Stephanie tried but she didn't manage very well. Old Sam shuffled around, doing his chores. He moved so slowly from place to place that it seemed he would never get done.

When the lamb was fed, Rosemary started to the orchard. There was another rope strung in another direction. She didn't hurry, she just wandered with the rope and Stephanie walked slowly beside her. The bees were buzzing and the breeze swayed the tree branches. Stephanie liked the sound.

"The plows will come next week, unless it rains too hard. They've already plowed the fields near the road," Rosemary said. "When Mr. Mitchell comes he lets me ride with him. I hold the wheel and he turns it. I wish he was here this week. Then you could ride. The ground smells so good when it's plowed."

Rosemary stooped and pulled a strand of tall grass. It squeaked as she pulled it through her fist.

"Some of the birds build nests in the grass. I wish they wouldn't. The plows can't miss all of them. I hate to think about nests under the tractor."

She looked serious. She was usually smiling and Stephanie didn't like it when she looked sad.

"When we get back, be sure to look up in under the sides of the garage roof. There are some mud nests. Daddy lifts me up so I can feel how they're shaped. Once a momma bird dived right at me. She thought I would hurt her babies."

"We have pigeons on the roof," Stephanie said, glad at last to have something to offer that might please Rosemary.

"You do? Are they yours?" Rosemary asked brightly.

"No. They just stay up there. Sometimes they sit outside the kitchen window. Momma leaves crumbs but they won't let us pet them."

"If you sit still and wait, they might. It takes a long time and you have to be very quiet," Rosemary suggested.

Stephanie tried to imagine it being quiet at her apartment. With children screaming, people fighting, horns honking, babies crying, it was never quiet there, even at night. This was the quiet place.

They had wandered in a circle and were near the garage again. Stephanie had scooped up a fist full of soil as they walked. It crumbled into fine particles between her fingers. She smelled it. Funny! How strange that dirt could almost smell clean.

Stephanie stopped to look at the bird nests. Old Sam brought a ladder so she could get close. She tapped one with her finger. It was so hard that she wondered if any baby bird would want to stay in it. But she peered inside and saw bits of string and other fluff. Birds weren't so dumb.

Sunshine came and went as great globs of clouds drifted across the sky. Rosemary surprised Stephanie again.

"It's getting cloudy. I can tell because I feel colder right away."

Mrs. Martin called them in for lunch—thick salami sandwiches and hard-boiled eggs.

"Our eggs are so fresh the hens almost lay them on the kitchen table," Dr. Martin said as he peeled one.

Rosemary began to giggle. She had a mouthful of egg and she looked so funny that Stephanie started to giggle too. They both tried to stop but another giggle would pop out and they'd start all over. Mrs. Martin tried to hush them but giggles are persistent. Finally the girls had to leave the table. No one was angry, but giggles bother some people so they ran upstairs to try to calm down.

Mrs. Martin came up later. "Miss Gigglepuss, I have a message for you," she said to Rosemary. By then the giggles were all worn out.

"Dr. Franklin called. He wants to see you to-morrow."

"Ohhhhh," Rosemary said with a moan. "Not while Stephanie is here! Please, Momma. It'll ruin the whole day. Please!"

Mrs. Martin sat on the bed, gathering Rose-mary's long hair in her hand.

"Dr. Franklin can't let people come just when they want to come. He has lots of people waiting to see him. What would happen if Daddy just sat around and waited for a sick animal to wander in for a checkup?"

Stephanie laughed hard. That was silly. She

could just see a pig waddling into the front room with a bellyache. But Rosemary was mad and pouting. She flopped back on her bed.

"I can go next week," she snapped.

"It only takes an hour or so. Stephanie can wait in the office or go to the store with me until you're done," Mrs. Martin said firmly.

"No, Momma, please! If I have to go, can't Stephanie stay here?"

Now Mrs. Martin looked almost angry. "Why should she stay here? That doesn't make sense, Rosemary."

"Please!" Rosemary seemed ready to cry.

Stephanie said quickly, "I'll stay here."

"That's kind of you, Stephanie, but we'll worry about that tomorrow," Mrs. Martin said. She left the room without her usual smile.

Rosemary said nothing for a long time. Stephanie sat on the window seat and looked at the green landscape which stretched for miles in front of her.

"Stephanie," Rosemary said in a small voice.

"Huh?" Stephanie answered without turning around.

"Are you mad at me?"

Stephanie faced her. "Why should I be?"

"Because I want you to stay here and not go to the Doctor's."

"I'm not mad." She hadn't even thought about being mad.

"I have a reason, but you might not understand it. Momma wouldn't understand."

"I don't care if I stay here," Stephanie said lightly.

"Can I tell you my reason?" Rosemary asked.

"I guess so." Stephanie didn't need any reason but she would listen.

Rosemary spoke slowly. "When I go to the Doctor he always says cheerful stuff like 'I wish I had your red hair,' or 'Give me some of your extra freckles for my little girl.' But I know it isn't funny when I have to go there. He's always trying to make me see again, but it never happens."

Rosemary put her face in her pillow. It was silent again.

"And I try to laugh for him. But I really want to cry. I always dream that he can make me see again."

She came to the window seat and sat next to Stephanie.

Stephanie wasn't sure she understood but she felt terrible. All this talk left a pain inside her. She wished the doctor had waited until next week, too. If Rosemary didn't want her to go, if it would make her unhappy, she wouldn't, that's all.

"I don't want to go. Honest. I want to stay here." Stephanie tried to sound natural. "I'll stay. O.K.?"

Rosemary tried to smile, but it just made Stephanie turn quickly away from those blue eyes, those blue eyes that saw nothing.

That evening, Rosemary said, "Come walk with me, please."

She took Stephanie's hand, tugging at her. Stephanie put on her coat. They went outside quickly, without even telling Mrs. Martin. The road was almost dark, a little frightening. Rosemary clung to Stephanie's hand and allowed herself to be led. The evening wind shoved its way through the old tall trees, making them creak and groan.

"Do you hate what you are?" Rosemary asked suddenly.

Stephanie felt that pain again, that hurt inside that had bothered her when Rosemary had almost cried.

"I don't hate anybody," Stephanie said quickly, hoping Rosemary wouldn't go on like this.

"No, I mean, hate being what you are? I do sometimes. I really hate it!" Rosemary pulled her hand free and put her fingers on her face. "It isn't fair to be blind. It isn't."

For a long dreadful moment, Stephanie thought Rosemary would cry—cry hard. She didn't know what she should do. Take her home? Try to talk about other things? What?

"People who know I'm blind talk about me. They think I don't hear but I do. Momma tries to keep them away but it doesn't change things. She tries to help but she can't do much."

Stephanie was miserable. She turned back toward the house. Mrs. Martin would know what to do. Or would she? Stephanie remembered that time in their own kitchen, when her mother tried to make her understand about ugly things. Her mother had tried to say good things, but it hadn't helped much.

"A lot of white people think I'm different, too," Stephanie said, her eyes darting from one shadow to the other. It was getting quite dark. "Because I'm black."

"I know. But that's not the same as being blind, is it? It doesn't make you really different like me." Rosemary's voice was shaky.

Suddenly Stephanie was angry. She could tell Rosemary a lot of things about being treated as different, about being black and trying to live in a world full of white people. She had to fight back the mean words which were at the very tip of her tongue. But it wasn't Rosemary's fault. Rosemary was her friend, and she didn't want to hurt her.

Rosemary was reaching out for, trying to catch hold of her hand again. Stephanie reached out, too. "Just because people think you're different doesn't mean you are," she said.

She headed for the house, moving as quickly as she could. She didn't like this whole thing—the darkness, the way they had been talking. She tried to think of something else, even something funny. But this wasn't the time for anything funny. She slipped her arm tightly around Rosemary's arm and they linked their hands together.

"Wait!" Stephanie told her as they came to the front steps. "It's the steps."

Rosemary stopped still and wiped her cheek with one hand.

"O.K. I know where I am. Thanks."

This time Rosemary smiled, really smiled.

As Stephanie sat on the back porch the next morning, the clock in the hall gonged ten times.

Rosemary and her parents had left at nine for the appointment with the eye doctor. Stephanie told them over and over she really didn't want to go, so they left her with Sam.

In the shadowed garage across the driveway, she saw something moving. She watched carefully. A cat was sneaking close to the ground. What was it doing? Stephanie got up and moved quietly to the open doors. The cat had vanished but she heard very small sounds coming from a rag pile near the workbench. She went closer. Just then the large cat reappeared in the doorway. In its mouth was a lump of fur. The cat headed right to the rags and Stephanie watched, fascinated, as the cat dropped the little thing. It was a kitten and there were at least four more already nestled in the rags. Maybe they had been born during the storm just as Rosemary had said.

Stephanie bent down. The mother cat curled herself next to the kittens and licked one of them over and over. Gently Stephanie slid her hand under one spotted kitten and lifted it. It was so warm. She touched it to her cheek and heard it purr. Its eyes were shut. She remembered how Rosemary had told her she could have a kitten to keep. She stroked it with one finger.

"No, I wouldn't take you or any other kitten

away from your mother," she whispered. "It's better for you here. Lots better."

She put the kitten down close to its mother and stood up. It would be fun to keep one. But she couldn't stand it if it got hurt or lost in the city streets.

Stephanie left the garage slowly and wandered over to watch Sam who was digging up the ground near the orchard. He was stooped over pulling up clumps of weeds. She tugged at some. It surprised her that they were so tough. She grabbed another one hard and it suddenly pulled free, plopping her in the dirt. Old Sam straightened himself.

"City gal, you don't have to work that hard," he said in his slow, creaky way. "You said you don't have a garden back home?" he asked leaning on his shovel.

"Our apartment doesn't have a yard," Stephanie said. Didn't people in the country know anything about the city?

"Don't always need a yard, child. Just fill a few pots with some good soil and raise you some onions. Do it on the porch."

"We don't have a porch either," Stephanie said, pulling on a sticky weed. She left it alone and moved to another one.

Sam put his shovel against the garage. He was chewing something and he spit. Stephanie had seen old men on the city street corners do the same thing. She didn't like it.

"Better tend that lamb. Ain't comin' too good," he muttered as he went toward the pens. Stephanie followed.

The lamb was under the shed roof. It huddled against the wooden slats, almost invisible. When it lifted its head Stephanie could see its eyes glisten. Then its head fell again. Old Sam went in and fussed around but he came out soon and shook his head.

"That one's not goin'a make it." He shuffled back to the garden plot.

Stephanie leaned against the pen wire, her fingers through the holes. She stared at the gray, ugly lump, the lamb named "Beautiful."

"You won't die, will you?" she whispered.

Rosemary loved the lamb and it just couldn't die. Stephanie crouched closer to the ground, trying to see it better.

"I'll love you too, if you try to get better. I'll pet you and feed you. I don't think you're ugly, honest. I'll love you like Rosemary does."

But the lamb lay still, its runny eyes shut.

Stephanie went back to the house. It seemed much bigger when no one was in it. She went in through the back porch and there were cookies on a plate in the kitchen. She took one and sat at the table. The dishes they would use for lunch were ready to be set out. Stephanie noticed that most of them were chipped. They had a delicate gold pattern but there were lots of cracks. The cup handles had been glued. That was a surprise, to discover that they were old and used.

She remembered her mother's words that unhappy afternoon in the apartment—"We have to use everything until it just won't work anymore." So Mrs. Martin had to use things until they were no good anymore, too.

Stephanie finished her cookie. She passed the old clock ticking loudly in the deserted house. The face of the clock was rusted, and hard to read. Pieces of wood around the edge had peeled away but it kept on ticking. It didn't seem to care if it was heard or not.

She wished Rosemary was back. She climbed the stairs slowly. On the third step there was a hole in the carpet that went right through to the wood. She looked down behind her. When she first came up these stairs on Saturday they looked very wide and fancy. But they were really sagging and old.

In the bedroom she sat on the window seat again. She raised the window but it took some time because the wood was swollen from the last rain. On the outside wall a vine wrapped around and around itself and hung against the screen. It was heavy with clusters of white flowers but not many leaves. They had a thick over-sweet smell that made her dizzy when she breathed deeply.

The white curtains stirred in the air, touching her shoulder. She pushed them aside. They were limp and delicate, but the edges were ragged, and the material was torn where the curtains bunched together. The blue bows that held the curtains in place were faded and ravelling.

Stephanie felt guilty looking at the torn places. She went to her bed and lay down, looking up at the ceiling. The flowered wallpaper covered the ceiling, too. But along the middle where the light hung, the paper had peeled away.

She turned over. She didn't want to see that ceiling. Then she realized that the blue bedspread was mended, stitched here and there. Near the bottom was a patch that didn't match the rest of it.

She sat up. She was getting a strange feeling. When she looked from place to place in the room, everything changed. The scratched and broken

things were everywhere. Even the mirror above
the dresser had black spots. It was just like the
night when Miss Bloom came.

"Stop it!" she said out loud. What was she
doing, she asked herself angrily, talking out loud
to nobody?

She heard a crunching on the gravel driveway.
They were back.

11

STEPHANIE ran to the open window. "Hi, hi!" she called.

Then she ran downstairs and out to the porch. Rosemary was coming up the steps with a package in her arms.

"Hi, we're back. Did you find any monsters or anything?" she asked with a grin.

"No, I just waited for you," Stephanie said, holding the door open.

They all had a good lunch and Rosemary showed Stephanie the collection of things in the package she had brought home. There were seed packets and mesh bags of bulbs, some flowers, some vegetables. After lunch Sam took all of it to the garden. All but one packet. He left one on top of the refrigerator.

In the garden the earth was folded back in neat rows. It reminded Stephanie of pieces of milk chocolate in the dime stores. Rosemary and Stephanie stayed with Sam for a long time while he planted seeds and set bulbs deep in the ground. He patted the soil like Rosemary patted the sick animals. His pale hands were very gentle.

Rosemary went to the pens and spoke to all the animals. Stephanie hoped Sam wouldn't say anything about Beautiful. She was glad he stayed near his garden.

"Here you go, little one," Rosemary said as she knelt next to the lamb with a feeding bottle. "You don't seem very hungry today. Maybe Sam already fed you." She set the bottle down and left the pen.

But Stephanie knew Sam hadn't fed the lamb. It just wasn't going to eat. Maybe it couldn't. She worried about that. Mrs. Martin asked them to help clean the car after she washed it down with the hose. It didn't look much better clean than it did dirty. Rosemary kept rubbing the sides and hood with a rag.

"If you rub hard it shines," she told Stephanie.

But there was no shine left on the blue paint. Stephanie used a little brush to sweep out the floor. The mat was pulled loose and she could see right down to the ground.

"Rosemary, why don't you and Stephanie go over to Bergermans' for some butter. I'm almost out," Mrs. Martin suggested.

"Want to go?" Rosemary called to Stephanie from the back of the garage.

"Sure," Stephanie called back.

Mrs. Martin spoke quietly to Stephanie as she shut the car door and rolled up the hose. "When you go, honey, keep an eye out for things that may have fallen on the path, just in case. O.K.?"

"I don't know where to go. Won't somebody come with us?" Stephanie was concerned.

"Rosemary knows every inch of the path to Bergermans' farm. Don't worry about her. You won't get lost, just watch out for things."

Together they followed the same path toward the stream but Rosemary turned uphill instead of down. Another rope was right there. It led off through the trees and Rosemary just went with it.

"There's a little creek along here. It's tiny and we can cross it easy," Rosemary said.

Sure enough a trickle of clear water ran out from under the logs and wandered off into the bushes again. All along its edge were white flowers set atop long, almost invisible stems.

"Do you want to try my rope?" Rosemary asked with a funny grin.

She stopped and held the rope away from herself. Stephanie paused. She was interested in the rope.

"O.K." Stephanie said, grinning too. She took hold of it.

"Now shut your eyes tight. And don't peek or it won't be fair. I'll wait here. You go ahead then turn around and come back."

Stephanie shut her eyes. She remembered that the path wound a little to the left, so she held the rope and stepped away. But as soon as she took a step, she wasn't sure if the path went left or right! She was tugging against the rope but it didn't stretch as far as it should. She let go, just for a second.

Squish! Her shoe sank into something wet and oozy. She opened her eyes. She was not on the path at all. She was standing in another little trickle of water that ran beside the opposite side of the path. Her tennis shoe was soaked!

"Are you coming back?" Rosemary called.

"Yes. I'm coming back," Stephanie answered. She grabbed the rope and headed for Rosemary. But she didn't close her eyes. She was embarrassed that she hadn't trusted the rope. And her foot was soaked because she hadn't.

"Did you do it? Did it work for you?" Rosemary was full of interest.

Stephanie wanted to say yes but she couldn't.

"I got wet. I dropped the rope and opened my eyes." She felt stupid.

"Oh, I'm sorry about that. There's another creek over there. I should have warned you. Most people can't use my rope. They just don't trust it."

Stephanie looked seriously at her friend, standing there with her hand around the rope. Rosemary trusted because she had to. Stephanie wondered why *she* couldn't trust, just for a few minutes.

They kept on the path, Stephanie in the lead. It was a wonderful walk, through trees wearing all kinds of blossoms. The sun filtered through the branches to the earth. Stephanie paused now and then to feel the spongy moss clinging to the northern, shadowed sides of the tree trunks. A rotten branch had fallen across the path. Stephanie told Rosemary to wait while she shoved it clear.

It wasn't far to the other farm. The hill that divided the Bergermans' place from the Martins' was heavily wooded, but small. Stephanie hadn't expected another farm to be so close. The trees ended and plowed fields lay in front of them. Rosemary's rope stopped at a white fence several yards beyond.

"This is the Bergermans'," Rosemary said, holding on to the fence post. "The barn is closest to us. The house is next to the big tree."

The nearby barn glistened white and Stephanie could see that it was being painted one side at a time. This farm was like others Stephanie had glimpsed from the fast moving bus. It was neat and tidy like another picture Miss Bloom might use with a poem.

It was many feet from the fence to the house. Stephanie was about to reach for Rosemary's hand when Rosemary called out.

"Hello. It's Rosemary. Hello."

There was no movement near the barn. The chickens made a racket but no one could be seen.

"Mrs. Bergerman is coming. I can hear her," Rosemary said.

The screen door on the side porch squeeked open and a tall, round faced woman came toward them. She walked like a man, with long heavy strides. And she had deep frown creases on her face.

"Most didn't hear you, child. I was turning the separator."

The woman had a strong voice, like a man, too. She took a firm hold on Rosemary's arm and led her to the house. Stephanie looked up, to smile at the woman. But the woman didn't look at her, not even once. Stephanie trotted to keep up and Rosemary stumbled. She couldn't move as quickly as the woman insisted.

At the porch the woman let go of Rosemary. Rosemary rubbed her arm and reached out for Stephanie.

"Mrs. Bergerman, this is my friend, Stephanie Harris. She's staying with us for a week," Rosemary said politely.

"So I heard," the woman answered. Her voice was sharp. She went up the steps. "Come along, Rosemary. I guess you came to fetch butter."

"Yes, m'am. Momma is all out," Rosemary said and began to go up the steps. Mrs. Bergerman stepped between Stephanie and Rosemary.

The woman looked hard at Stephanie. "Wait outside. Your shoes are muddy."

"Oh, that's all right, isn't it? I might be muddy, too," Rosemary said and stepped back. But the woman grabbed her and took her in. The door slammed shut. Stephanie stood alone. She looked down at her shoes. They were muddy and even her socks were wet. But Rosemary's shoes were muddy, too. She went back down the steps. She knew she should wait right there for Rosemary. But she didn't. She went to the barn and leaned against the wall. She kept her head down, staring at her feet. Muddy shoes. Muddy shoes. She kept thinking that over and over until she heard the screen door open again. Then she looked up.

The woman led Rosemary back toward the fence. Rosemary was moving her free hand around in the air.

"Where's Stephanie? Where is she?"

The woman put Rosemary's hand on the fence, then turned on her heel and marched away. "She's around. Just call her."

Stephanie stood still, glaring at the woman's back as she returned to her neat, tidy house and shut her noisy screen door. Muddy shoes, muddy shoes! She gritted her teeth.

"Stephanie? Where are you?" Rosemary was calling for her, both hands waving in the air.

Stephanie went to her side and took hold of her hand.

"Here I am," she said quietly.

"Gosh, I was worried. Come on, let's get out of here."

Rosemary took the rope and moved swiftly back to the path. Stephanie looked behind them, at the neat, white farm. She could almost feel two small eyes watching them leave. She had to hurry to keep up with Rosemary.

"I'm sorry that Mrs. Bergerman didn't invite you inside," Rosemary said as she walked. "She keeps that house like a hospital, everything scrubbed like the dickens. Momma says you could eat off of her floors, they're so clean. She has a fit about mud."

Stephanie frowned. She stamped her "muddy" shoes on the ground. That woman had other reasons for not inviting her into the house. And Stephanie had seen her reasons in her squinty eyes. Stephanie could have told Rosemary what she was thinking but what good would it do? It wasn't Rosemary's fault.

The butter was rich, yellow and smooth. Mrs. Martin put it in a special dish. They had warmed their hands at the stove as soon as they came in. The kitchen was cheerful, but Stephanie still had a frown on her face. Mrs. Martin didn't notice.

"Mrs. Bergerman said the butter costs more

starting next week. She said feed costs more for the cows," Rosemary told her mother as she warmed her hands.

"Well, everything is higher so I expected that," Mrs. Martin said with a shrug.

"Stephanie didn't get to see their scrubbed house. Mrs. Bergerman had her wait outside because of muddy shoes. You know how fussy she is," Rosemary said.

Mrs. Martin turned around slowly and looked right at Stephanie. She looked at her shoes. Then she looked at Rosemary's shoes. Both were mud caked.

And Mrs. Martin bit her lip. She stood next to Stephanie and smoothed her loose hair back from her face.

"Some neighbors aren't quite like we want them to be," she said softly to Stephanie. She understood, about the shoes and about the round-faced, frowning woman with the white house. She understood.

12

THE NEXT DAY began with jobs. Sam was working on a pipe that leaked in the kitchen. Mrs. Martin cleaned cupboards. She wore a fresh apron and her hair was tied back with a piece of pink yarn.

In the hen house Stephanie discovered there were eggs that had been already laid in the early part of the day.

"Can I pick one?" she asked Rosemary.

"Pick one? It sounds like fruit on a tree," Rosemary said with a laugh. "Better ask the hen first if you can take it," she teased.

Stephanie hesitated, then reached for the egg. The hen struck at her with its beak.

"Ooops!" Stephanie said, stepping back.

"I told you to ask first. No, I'm just kidding. All you have to do is grab. She'll squawk and flap her wings but that's all."

Stephanie moved back to the straw nest and grabbed quickly. She got the egg and the hen hopped to the ground, complaining in chicken talk. She carefully put the egg in the metal bucket.

A horn sounded out on the main road.

"Let's get the mail," Rosemary said, pulling Stephanie with her.

They went to the mailbox bundled in their coats. It was blustery and the wind made their noses cold but it was a good, fresh feeling. Dr. Martin drove past them on his way to care for some animal on another farm. He honked and they yelled, "Goodbye."

There were two magazines in the box and one letter. It said "Miss Stephanie Harris" right on the front. Stephanie could see her name on it even though Rosemary held it.

"That letter is for me," she said quietly, touching the stubby envelope.

"It is? Hey, that's good. Take it."

Stephanie held the letter tightly. She wanted to open it right there in the windblown road, but it was too cold to stand around reading. They hur-

ried back to the warm house and gave the magazines to Mrs. Martin.

"Stephanie got a letter," Rosemary told her
mother.

"That's nice. Is it from your folks?" Mrs. Martin asked as she thumbed through one magazine.

"Yes," Stephanie said, smiling at the letter. It
was the first letter she had ever received. Sometimes there was mail with her name on it at home,
but they were just ads that wanted her parents to
buy something. Not real letters. Stephanie stood
around. Should she read her letter to everybody?
She didn't know.

Mrs. Martin said, "Hang up your coats, girls.
Maybe it will warm up later and you can go out
again."

So they went up to the bedroom. Stephanie put
the letter on her bed and watched Rosemary brush
her hair.

"Would you like to hear my letter?" Stephanie
asked finally.

"If you want me to," Rosemary said, tipping her
head as she always did when she wasn't certain
about things.

"Yea, it's o.k. if you want to hear it." Stephanie
picked at the flap with her fingernail. She didn't

want to tear the letter inside. Rosemary sat with her feet tucked under her. Stephanie unfolded her letter and began to read.

"Dear Sugar Bee,"

"Sugar Bee? Who's Sugar Bee?" Rosemary asked quickly.

Stephanie could have bitten her own tongue! What a dumb thing to do. She had read her own nickname out loud like that. Now she was stuck.

"Who's Sugar Bee? Is that you?" Rosemary leaned toward Stephanie.

Stephanie squirmed. She didn't want to explain about that miserable name. But she wasn't going to lie either.

"That's what my mother calls me." Stephanie sagged all over.

"Don't you like it?" Rosemary smiled from ear to ear. "Gee, I think it's perfect!"

"My real name is Stephanie. They call me Stephanie at school." Stephanie's voice was low and heavy. How could she explain that a nickname bothered her so much? She drew a long breath and went on with the letter.

"We miss you, honey. The neighbors ask about you. They are all waiting to hear about your fine week in the country. Olive came to play yesterday.

She forgot that you were gone. Remember the lady who cleans machines at the laundermat? She had a baby girl and is very happy. Miss Bloom came to visit last night. Poppa was across the hall so he missed her. She thinks you are a very special . . ."

Stephanie hesitated. It sounded stuck-up to read good things about yourself, so she skipped that part.

"I found a coat for you. You'll like it. It will be a good Easter surprise for you when you come home. I hope you are polite. Be a good girl. Remember to thank the Martin family for everything. We will meet you Saturday evening at the bus depot. Be careful. Love from Mother." She really only whispered the last few words. They were special.

Saturday. It was getting closer and closer, Stephanie thought.

Rosemary moved over to Stephanie's bed and sat down.

"Are you getting homesick?"

"I miss my mother and father," Stephanie admitted.

"Do you miss your friends?" Rosemary asked quietly.

"Not really. It's nice here."

"I'm your friend too," Rosemary went on.

"I hope so," Stephanie said, looking right at Rosemary. But it was hard when Rosemary couldn't look back. It made her sad.

"Can I tell you something?" Rosemary tipped her head, uncertain.

"Sure."

"I love your nickname. I really do." She shook her finger in the air. "But I can tell you don't like it and I promise not to use it."

Stephanie sighed. She didn't really hate it. It just sounded so—well, so dumb. It didn't ever sound as fine as Stephanie.

"Do you want to know why I like it?" Rosemary asked.

"I guess so."

"Because it sounds like you. Names should sound like the person. And Sugar Bee fits you. When you say Stephanie, it could sound like someone who won't play or won't get dirty while you're having fun. You know what I mean?"

Stephanie didn't really. It was odd to hear anyone say that they liked "Sugar Bee" for a name. It was strange to have someone care about how your name sounds.

Rosemary kept on. "I don't have a nickname. Did you notice?"

Stephanie HAD noticed.

"Daddy used to call me 'Rosie' or 'Rosieposy.' You know how fathers can pick silly names."

Yes, Stephanie knew.

"Well, I think roses are the prettiest flowers of all. And my name is just Rose with Mary on the end. So I asked everyone to please just call me Rosemary. And they do." She smiled.

"How do you know roses are pretty?" Stephanie said without thinking. And as soon as the words were out, she knew how unkind they were.

Rosemary smoothed her hair back from her face and Stephanie wished desperately that she hadn't opened her mouth.

"I didn't go blind until I was seven. I'm twelve and it's been a long time since I saw roses but I do remember. Momma's roses get so big that one of them could fill both of your hands."

Stephanie sat very still. Rosemary held her hands cupped before her, as though they were sheltering a delicate rose at that very moment.

"Roses smell better than any perfume, even when they wilt. I pick one fresh every morning during the late spring and put it in that skinny vase on the hall table. You can always tell when there's a rose in the house, even from the front room."

Rosemary had sprawled on Stephanie's bed,

patting the blue bedspread with her fingers.

"And I remember everything in this room. The way the curtains puff out in the middle and the way they're tied up there with blue bows. The wallpaper with curly vines and flowers. And I remember the color of my hair. I guess it's just about as red as hair can get. Yours is black, isn't it?"

"Yes," Stephanie said, very softly.

"And your skin is dark brown too, huh?"

"Yes."

Stephanie almost couldn't stand it. To have Rosemary talk about things she used to see, to talk about roses and curtains and red hair, when she couldn't ever see them again. Stephanie felt tears coming.

"Can I touch your face, Stephanie? I'll know you better if I can. Then I can make a picture of you in my mind. The doctor says that's a good way to learn. Can I?"

Stephanie almost said "no, no," because the idea scared her. But she struggled with herself and said "Sure" in a shaky, broken voice.

Rosemary stood up quickly. She put out both hands and touched Stephanie's face.

"Are you crying?" She was startled.

Stephanie shook her head hard, but the tears were there.

"Did I say something wrong?" Rosemary was terribly worried.

Stephanie still shook her head.

Rosemary's arms grew stiff.

"Are you crying because . . . because I'm blind?"

Stephanie hung her head. She whispered, "Yes."

"Well, don't!" Rosemary blurted, suddenly changed. "Don't feel sorry for me! I'm blind and I'll always be blind. But don't cry about it. Do you hear?"

Stephanie didn't move. She was afraid to speak, afraid to get up and walk away. She just stared, wide-eyed, as Rosemary walked directly to the window and sat on the seat, her hands gripping the sill.

"You can see me, can't you?" Rosemary said sharply, her head held high. "Sure you can. You can see anything you want to. I can't. That's the only difference between us. So don't you ever feel sorry for me. I don't feel sorry for anybody else." She threw her hands out wide.

"Since you can see, look at this room. Look at it!" She told Stephanie. "It's full of old stuff, isn't it?"

Stephanie kept staring at Rosemary. She was so sorry that she had caused this outburst. It was awful. She kept telling Rosemary to stop, telling her over and over, but only in her mind.

"My folks keep the old things. They know I remember them. They stay in this old house, because I know how to live here. I know how to run around in it. My mother keeps everything just like it was when I was seven, when I could see. They use all their money for that Doctor. And he can't do anything!" Rosemary was standing. Her face twisted up and she started to cry.

Stephanie went to her and Rosemary almost pushed her away. Stephanie suddenly had to talk, to say things that were crowding inside her.

"I'm not sorry for you. I didn't mean to make you cry. Please."

Rosemary's hands were tight in her lap and her shoulders were hunched in anger. Stephanie stamped her own foot.

"Listen! I'm not sorry for you. Understand? I don't even have a house to live in. It's an old rotten apartment, full of bugs. And even rats! And my mother gets sick there. My poppa hasn't got one of those college things. He doesn't have lots of money either. He almost couldn't let me come here 'cause he didn't have enough money."

Stephanie caught her breath. It was all wrong, shouting at each other like this, but she just had to say her share and get rid of things that hurt her, too.

Rosemary stood up slowly. She brushed the tears from her face and then reached out.

"Oh gosh, Stephanie. I'm sorry. I started all this mess. Honest, I'm sorry." Her fingers touched Stephanie's cheek.

Stephanie didn't turn away. She closed her eyes and Rosemary traced her face ever so lightly with her slender fingers.

"Now I can see you," Rosemary said. "Now I know you're really my friend."

But Stephanie didn't know. Were they really friends? Was it possible to be a real friend to someone who lived in such a different way? Painful questions filled her head.

Yip and Yap set up a howl outside. It was an announcement that someone was coming up the driveway. Both girls could hear the clatter of the Silver Dairy Truck. Rosemary went to the bedroom door. She turned to Stephanie.

"Will you come? Maybe they brought fresh cottage cheese. It's really good."

Stephanie looked at Rosemary for a long moment, then without answering, followed her downstairs.

13

THE RATTLING yellow truck pulled over beside the pens. One man got out. Dr. Martin was inside the pen and Mrs. Martin had bent down to pick up the lamb's feeding bowl. The dairy man went to the back of the truck and lowered the tailgate. He pulled another box to the edge and went into the pen.

Stephanie stood back. She knew something was wrong.

Rosemary made her way to the open pen door.

"Daddy, is the lamb going home today? Is it better already?" She tipped her head back, puzzled, for the lamb had been so sick.

"Are you taking Beautiful home today, Mr. Silver? I helped take care of her, didn't I, Daddy?"

Rosemary kept moving, feeling her way into the pen. She held one hand out, searching for the lamb. Dr. Martin looked at the man and at Mrs. Martin. He took Rosemary's outstretched hand.

"Honey, your Beautiful was just too sick. She couldn't get well. We both tried to help her but she just couldn't make it," he said quietly.

Rosemary stood very still. She held out her other hand.

"Can I pet her once more?"

Mr. Silver had picked up the little lamb to put it in the box. He stepped over to Rosemary and touched the lamb to her fingers.

"I loved you, little one," she said.

Stephanie was standing outside the pen. She turned and ran. She ran all the way beyond the driveway and into the trees where Rosemary's rope was hanging. She stumbled along the path and pushed her way through the bushes, toward the little stream.

Birds had clustered at the edge of the water. They fluttered away in fright. Squirrels on top of the rock scampered up a tree. Stephanie slumped against the rock and put her head in her arms. She cried and cried.

After a while it was very quiet. The birds came

back to drink. Squirrels ran halfway down the tree trunk to see if they were alone. Stephanie was still sitting against the rock. She had not moved. Her head was down and her arms were wrapped around her knees. She didn't cry anymore but she didn't leave.

The ugly lamb had died. Why? Rosemary loved it. It should have gotten better. It should have! It should! She rocked back and forth, feeling empty.

"Stephanie."

She heard a voice, at the top of the hill above the stream.

"Stephanie, where are you?"

It was Rosemary. Stephanie could see her through the trees, her red hair bright against the greening leaves. She called out again.

"Stephanie, are you on the rock?"

Stephanie knew she should answer but she didn't. She held her head down and hoped Rosemary would follow the rope back home. But Rosemary left the rope tree and started down the slope alone, clutching out at the bushes. Stephanie looked up quickly. That was dangerous, trying to grab the bushes. Stephanie got up and climbed toward Rosemary. They met at a crooked tree that lay sideways against the hill.

"Here, take my hand," Stephanie said.

She led Rosemary carefully back to the rock. They both sat for a long time and said nothing. Then Rosemary raised her head high, listening.

"Hear that?" she asked Stephanie. "Do you hear that buzzing?" She pointed across the stream toward the soft sound.

Stephanie could hear it.

"Those are honey bees. Just like your name. Sugar Bee. They're all over the place in the spring. I'll bet they're making a mountain of honey."

Stephanie could see a pink fringed bush bending low from a heavy burden of blossoms. The sound seemed to come from there. She looked back at Rosemary. There were no tears on her cheeks. Her eyes didn't even look like she had been crying. Why not? It was her lamb that died. Why didn't she cry about it, if she really loved the ugly thing?

"Some people are afraid of bees," Rosemary said. "I'm not. They never bother me. Momma says they're afraid of my red hair." She laughed a little.

Stephanie said nothing. She felt so bad that the lamb had died. Why didn't Rosemary feel bad too?

"Momma said you ran away from the pen. I

didn't know that you were gone. I was waiting for the truck to leave. Did you run away . . . to cry?" Rosemary asked gently.

"Yes!" Stephanie had an angry sound to her voice.

"I know how you feel. I used to cry when the animals died. But Daddy said God doesn't want animals to suffer. So they just sleep and don't suffer anymore. Some of them get better. Lots of them do. But the lamb . . . my Beautiful, was just too sick."

Rosemary kept her lips tight together and shut her eyes for a moment. Then she stood and held out her hand.

"Will you help me cross the stream?"

Stephanie shook her head. She didn't want to lead Rosemary. It might not work, they might slip and fall. She didn't get up.

"No," she said glumly.

"Don't worry," Rosemary smiled. "I'll follow you carefully. Just go slow and it'll be o.k."

"You'll get wet," Stephanie said slowly.

"I'll take off my shoes. You take off yours, too. Then it won't matter if we get our feet wet. I want to show you something."

Rosemary bent down and took off her shoes,

tucking her socks in them. Stephanie hesitated.
Then she took off hers, too. The ground was
chilled. They joined hands. Stephanie glanced up
and down the stream, trying to find a narrow
place. There were many small rocks. It would be
easy enough for her to cross, but hard to lead Rosemary.

One step at a time she put her feet in the thick
sandbed of the stream. It was COLD! Rosemary
squealed when she stepped in. With four steps
they were across and their feet were throbbing
from the icy water. It almost hurt.

"Look for a tree with vines hanging all over it.
Do you see it?" Rosemary asked. "Then we'll go
around it and down the hill a bit."

Stephanie led the way, her feet throbbing. The
grass felt slick. She was staring at the ground so she
wouldn't lead Rosemary into stickers or stones.
There were tiny yellow flowers everywhere. She
hated to step down because they were underfoot
like a delicate carpet.

There was a small field ahead. In the center of
it, where the sunshine was full, sat six white boxes.
And they were humming!

"We won't go any closer," Rosemary said, holding back. "Those boxes are Daddy's beehives. He

built them when I was little. I used to come here
with him when he gathered the honey. We wore
hats with net all over and long heavy gloves. We
put string around the bottom of our pants. It
really looked silly. But bees can get awful mad
when you bother the hives."

Stephanie listened. The humming grew loud
and then faded and grew loud again. She didn't
see any big bunch of bees, just a few here and
there. But there was sure a lot of noise.

"I don't come here much anymore. Daddy lets
Sam gather the honey now and Sam can't be both-
ered dragging me around when he's working. But
I wanted to come here with you. Know why?"
Rosemary asked with a grin.

Stephanie shrugged. She didn't know why. She
was still brooding about the dead lamb.

"I wanted you to see these hives, so you'd know
about our bees. Remember the honey we have at
supper? It came from here. There's lots of clover
in the fields and clover honey is the best. So, now
when I eat honey or hear the bees I can think
about you."

"About me?" Stephanie muttered.

"Uhuh. Because I love your name. Your other
name. Sugar Bee. I know. It's a secret and you

don't like it. But I do. And I'll keep it to myself. Do you mind?"

Stephanie looked at Rosemary. If that name pleased her, if she really liked it, maybe it wasn't such a bad name after all. The beehives glistening white in the fresh green field, with a blanket of yellow blossoms—it was as pretty as any picture Miss Bloom ever had.

"Do you mind?" Rosemary asked again, her face serious.

"I guess not. If you like it, it's o.k."

They both smiled.

Way beyond the stream they heard a call. It was Dr. Martin. He was making his way down the hill, searching.

"Rosemary!" he called as loud as he could.

"Over here, Daddy," Rosemary called back.

With Stephanie leading, they went back to the place where they had crossed the stream. Dr. Martin stretched his legs and was over the water in one step. He looked worried.

"Where did you two go? Rosemary, you shouldn't ever go this far away. Don't you know that?" He sounded angry but Stephanie thought he was more worried than angry.

"I just wanted Sug . . ." She stopped quickly. "I

wanted to show Stephanie the beehives. She never saw any before."

"O.K., Miss Martin. You've explored enough for today. Hang on and we'll get back to the house. Your mother is waiting."

He turned around and crouched to the ground. He pulled Rosemary's arms over his shoulders. She wrapped her legs around his middle and held on. She was rather big for this but Dr. Martin carried her easily.

Stephanie gathered up their shoes and they all headed home. She gazed over her shoulder at the little field. It was something she wanted to remember, for a long time. It was a poem place.

The next day was Good Friday. They all went into town early, to the store. It was a comfortable old place, its walls hung with countless things Stephanie had never seen before. Leather gear for horses, farm tools, materials by the bolt stacked on shelves, boxes and boxes of merchandise, some opened, some still sealed. A fascinating place.

Rosemary and Stephanie sat on chairs at the rear of the store while Mrs. Martin picked out her groceries and other goods. The lady who owned the store came over to Rosemary and whispered something in her ear.

Rosemary said, "Oh, good," then reached out for Stephanie. "Come on. Mrs. Mullen found something I needed."

The three of them went behind a wooden counter. Mrs. Mullen took a flat sack from a shelf. She slipped out a flowery card and put it in Rosemary's hand. Rosemary traced all over it with her fingertips. The flower pattern was raised and the words had a fuzzy surface. It read "Blessed Easter to Mother." Mrs. Mullen read it in a whisper.

"It's perfect," Rosemary whispered back. "I'd like to sign it."

"Sure, darlin," Mrs. Mullen chuckled and reached in her apron pocket for a pencil. Rosemary laid the card on the counter and held the edge of it with her one hand. She wrote her name. Stephanie stared at the card. Rosemary couldn't see yet she could write. It was a rather crooked name, but anyone could read it.

"Is that o.k.?" Rosemary asked her.

"Gosh, yes," Stephanie said, with a surprised voice.

"I can write anything, you know," Rosemary said with a slight grin. "I just have to keep at it so I don't forget how."

She opened her purse and handed Mrs. Mullen a quarter.

"Here. And thank you, Mrs. Mullen," she said.

The heavyset woman winked at Stephanie and then went to the front of the store to help Mrs. Martin. Mrs. Martin called to the girls.

"I have to pick up some things at the cleaners. Be right back. Just wait for me." She left the store. Stephanie would have liked to wander around, looking at the odd collection of things in the high glass showcases, but she stayed next to Rosemary.

Stephanie noticed someone near the corner. A thin-faced blond boy peeked around a stack of crates. He had large eyes and ears that almost looked like flaps glued to the side of his head. He made his way up one big crate and sprawled on top, staring at Stephanie.

' Hi, Rosemary," he said in a childish chirp. But he wasn't looking at Rosemary. He kept staring at Stephanie.

"Hi, Matt," Rosemary answered. "You better get down from there. Mrs. Mullen will slap your bottom."

She knew he was perched above them because his voice came from high up.

Rosemary whispered to Stephanie. "That's Matthew. His father owns the gas station. He's six and a real pest!"

"This is Stephanie, Matt. She's visiting us," Rosemary said.

"Yea," Matt grunted. "She's a nigger."

Stephanie jerked. She tried not to, she tried to look at the floor and not see the boy staring at her.

"No! She's not!" Rosemary's answer was sharp and loud. She grabbed Stephanie's hand and held it so hard it hurt.

"My dad say's she's a nigger," little Matt whined. "My dad says so."

"Stephanie is my friend! She's a Negro, Matthew!" Rosemary was fiercely angry.

Matt slid down from the crate and poked his head around the corner. He stuck out his tongue and popped his eyes wide.

"Nigger," he snickered and ran out of the store.

"You brat!" Rosemary yelled after him. "You little brat!"

She stood up suddenly and threw her hands out in front of her. She bumped into the crates and for a second Stephanie thought they would tumble down and hit them. She jumped up and pulled Rosemary away. Rosemary hung on to Stephanie's arm, turning her head back and forth, trying to remember just where they were standing. She was confused. She had lost her sense of direction.

"Where's Momma? Where's our car?" she asked in a shaky voice.

Stephanie led her carefully out the front door of the store. A few yards beyond the store was a low rock wall and Matt was sitting there. He jumped down when they came out and ran into the little office of the gas station. He climbed on top of an old desk and pushed his face against the glass.

Stephanie glared at him. She wanted to yell something mean and nasty. She knew what words to use. She heard them almost every day in the city streets. But she held on to Rosemary instead and headed for the old blue car.

Mrs. Martin wasn't there. Stephanie looked up and down the road, at the small shops. She couldn't see her anywhere. Rosemary was fumbling for the door handle. She jerked the rear door open and sat down hard on the seat.

"That brat! That darn brat, brat, brat!" Rosemary said over and over as she kicked her foot against the front seat.

Stephanie sat beside her. They both slumped down. Mrs. Martin's head suddenly appeared at the window. She seemed startled to find them in the car.

"Well, here you two are. I thought you were

going to wait in the store. Did you get tired of waiting?"

Her voice was light and cheerful, as always. Stephanie just looked away and said nothing. Rosemary popped up and leaned over into the front seat.

"Oh, Momma! That brat, that brat Matt . . ." She was so mad that she stuttered.

Mrs. Martin grinned as she put the dry cleaned clothes on the seat. "What did he do this time? He's a real tease, Stephanie," she started to say.

Stephanie stared out the window. She wished they were gone, back at the house, away from the store.

"No, Momma. He didn't just tease. That little stinker!" Rosemary was almost yelling.

"Now, listen, young lady. Mind your manners!" Mrs. Martin said as she got behind the wheel and closed the door. "Matt is just a little boy."

"He's a stupid little brat, that's what he is! In the store he called Stephanie a . . . a . . ." Rosemary stopped. The word was hard to say. "He called her a name," she said in a low voice.

Mrs. Martin turned around and faced the girls. Her face was serious, too.

"Oh?" she paused. "What did he say?"

Rosemary squirmed and wrinkled her face.

She didn't want to use that awful, cruel word.

"Did he call you a nigger, Stephanie?" Mrs. Martin asked softly.

Stephanie turned and looked right at Mrs. Martin. "Yes," she said and looked away again.

"I'm sorry about that, Stephanie," Mrs. Martin continued. "Please don't put all the blame on Matt. He's just a boy. He only repeats what he hears. Can you understand that?"

Stephanie didn't answer. She just wanted to go, to have the noise of the car keep them from talking any more.

"This ice cream won't keep long. We'd better get home," Mrs. Martin said as she turned the key and started the sluggish motor.

The car rolled away. Rosemary was silent. Stephanie shoved herself in one corner. Mrs. Martin seemed very busy with the steering wheel and no one said a word.

Back home again there was a sadness over the three of them. Mrs. Martin went up the front stairs slowly and disappeared into the house. Rosemary sat on the porch chair and banged her foot against the railing.

Stephanie felt miserable. The little blond boy had been able to ruin the whole day with just one word. Stephanie slumped at the bottom of the steps making little *x*'s in the dirt with a twig.

Nigger was such an old word. She had heard it often enough. Other children and grown people had spit that word at her and her parents. She was almost used to it. Once in a while, black people themselves used the word to joke with each other. It made a sad, grim kind of joke. On her street hatred took on a lot of shapes and sounds. Men yelled at men, kids hurt other kids, all for nothing but hate.

Now when she looked up at Rosemary, sitting alone in that peeling wicker chair, Stephanie's heart was really sad. She could tell that that stupid word had hurt Rosemary, too. Maybe more than it hurt her.

She went up the stairs and took her friend's hand.

"Can we go for a walk?"

Rosemary tipped her head, uncertain.

"I guess," she said.

In the hall Mrs. Martin paused to watch them as they went toward the shadowed orchard. There were tears in her eyes.

The guide rope hung slack. This time Stephanie would guide Rosemary, not the rope. She decided to cross through the tall grass between the trees rather than walk beside the plowed rows. The grass was damp and smelled fresh. Here and there tall evergreens spread their thick branches like skirts against a peach-tinged sunset. Round rosy clouds took a stately stroll across the sky. With their free hands both girls set the long grass swishing.

"Don't look like that, please," Stephanie finally said. She asked it as a favor, like children beg from their mother.

Rosemary rubbed her face and tried to make a smile. But it wasn't a real one.

"I'm mad. I'm really mad. That brat made me so mad!"

Rosemary stopped still, lifted her head and suddenly yelled as loud as she could, "Matthew is a brat!"

Stephanie was startled at first. It sounded absolutely silly, standing in the peaceful orchard, yelling at a skinny boy miles away. Then she giggled. Just a tiny bit, but it was enough. Rosemary caught her breath and giggled, too. And they started to march through the bending grass, stomping their feet and sing-songing together.

"Matt is a brat! Matt is a brat!"

It was just as silly as the yelling but for some strange reason it made them feel better.

There was a loud thrashing in a tree above them. Stephanie threw her arms over her head. Rosemary wasn't afraid.

"It's just an old owl. Hunting for mice. They sit on a branch and watch. They can grab a mouse right off the ground."

As they stood quietly, Stephanie heard the small sounds of evening. Chickens clucking, frogs grumping somewhere, the flutter of doves settling on a limb. The quietness, the peace of the place took the shape of words in her mind. She found herself letting them become almost a poem.

"Do you have a best friend?" Rosemary asked.

"Mary Lou Edwards. She's in my grade."

"Is she fun?"

Stephanie shrugged. "I guess so. She's always asking questions. Some dumb ones. But she's o.k."

"What do you do together?" Rosemary was holding her hand and swinging it high and wide.

"We walk to school, part way. She lives closer than I do. We eat lunch together."

"Does she stay overnight at your house and stuff like that?"

"Yes, sometimes. But not much." Stephanie didn't want to explain that there wasn't much space for anyone else in their cramped rooms.

"Did your mother worry about you coming to stay with us?" Rosemary leaned against a tree and Stephanie waited for her to decide to walk on.

"Nope. She was glad."

"Is that friend . . . what's her name?" Rosemary forgot.

"Mary Lou Edwards," Stephanie answered.

"Is Mary Lou black?"

"Yes."

"Do you have friends who aren't black?" Rosemary was pulling a long blade of grass between her fingers. The squeak made Stephanie wrinkle her face. So did the question. It was kind of dumb, really, she thought.

"Sure I do. Olive is Japanese. The kids across the hall are white. Lots of kids."

"Do you like your black friends better than Olive or the others?" Rosemary asked the question easily, but Stephanie was uneasy.

"I like a lot of kids. Don't you?" Stephanie gave her an impatient look.

"Is it more fun to be with your black friends than it is to be with me?"

"No!" she blurted. Her voice was a little strong and nervous.

"Gee, are you mad, Stephanie? I didn't mean to get you mad." Rosemary took hold of both her hands. "I just hoped you'd tell me about your friends, that's all."

Friends. Stephanie paused. "My poppa says friends are hard to find and harder to keep."

"I don't have many friends," Rosemary said with a small sadness in her own voice.

Stephanie stopped. That surprised her.

Stephanie almost asked why not. But she caught herself just in time. It wouldn't be a good question.

"Farms are far apart. Kids can't run next door, like in town. And I sure can't." Rosemary's head drooped a little. "Most kids don't want to be stuck with someone who's blind. It's a bother."

"No, it isn't!" Stephanie said quickly, surely.

Rosemary lifted her head and she smiled. Just a tiny bit at first, then a real special smile.

"Honest?"

"Honest!" Stephanie said. And she meant it.

"Then we'll stay friends, won't we?" Rosemary asked.

"Sure. I want to. If you do. . . ." Stephanie waited.

"Good! Let's go in. It's freezing out here." Rosemary shivered and they quickly moved toward the distant house. The amber colored windows, lighted from the inside, made it glow. It was waiting for them, warm and comfortable.

When they went up to bed Stephanie saw a small white box on her pillow. She picked it up.

"Is this your box, Rosemary?" She went across the room to Rosemary, who was taking off her shoes.

Rosemary took the box in her hands and shook her head no. Then she grinned.

"It's not mine. It's yours. Isn't there a name on it?"

Stephanie looked again. Her name was written in small, neat letters on the top of the box.

"Yea! It's my name. What's in it?"

Rosemary laughed. "*I* know what it is. Best way for you to find out is just open it."

Stephanie sat down and carefully opened the box. Nestled inside was a delicate artificial egg. It was white with pink and light green rippled trimming. Stephanie lifted it out and held it up. One end was open and within the lovely egg was something else. A tiny figure was standing up in the center. Rosemary moved beside Stephanie on the bed.

"It's an egg, a fancy one," Stephanie said.

"I know. Momma told me she was getting it. What's inside?"

Stephanie peered back into the egg. She really didn't know what the figure was supposed to be. It could be a dog or a goat or . . .

"Well, it's white and sorta bumpy all over, with little ears and blue eyes," she said uncertainly.

"It's a lamb! Perfect!" Rosemary clapped her hands. "Momma got a lamb like 'Beautiful.' That's perfect."

Rosemary was delighted. Stephanie looked again. It COULD be a lamb. But it didn't look anything like the miserable lamb that died in that pen.

"It's pretty, really pretty," Stephanie said. She meant the whole frosty white egg.

"Great! Now you have a lamb to remember my little lamb by." Rosemary was so sure. She was pleased that there was another "Beautiful." Stephanie wouldn't dream of telling her otherwise.

Stephanie put the egg in its box and even after the lights were out, she reached over to touch it. The gift was a good ending to a troubled day. Her mother would love it, too. It would be something very lovely to keep for remembering.

14

BREAKFAST on Saturday morning was almost a feast. There were three kinds of doughnuts, juice and strawberries from the freezer, sausage and bacon. A bowl of scrambled eggs was crowded next to a stack of buttered toast.

Rosemary and Stephanie had been up early, almost before the chickens. But a rooster managed to crow from the fence while they dressed.

Rosemary had pulled her mother aside and whispered to her. Mrs. Martin gave her something from the top of the refrigerator. Rosemary put it in her pocket. Stephanie didn't try to look. It wouldn't be polite.

Dr. Martin had been outside at the pens and he had a red nose. The day was wet and cold. But the clouds were racing away and the sun promised to take charge of things very soon.

"What a breakfast!" Dr. Martin said heartily as they all seated themselves. "This is food suited to presidents or kings."

He held his fork and knife upright like it sometimes shows in paintings of kings.

Mrs. Martin smiled.

"But of course! I have a house full of royalty. A king, a knight and two princesses. This is a castle, not a farmhouse, my good King." And she bowed, spreading her checkered apron like a gown.

Rosemary giggled and flopped her napkin on top of her head.

"Where's my crown? The diamond one?" she asked with her chin stuck way up.

Stephanie put her napkin on her head too. She tapped Rosemary on the shoulder.

"I threw it away. It got dirty," she said in the same silly voice.

"Oh, bones! Now I'll have to use the golden one. And it's so clunky...."

"Hold. Silence!" said Dr. Martin, in a pretend gruff voice. "I demand silence at this royal table. Or I'll put you both in the dungeon for giggling in front of the king."

The girls sputtered, their hands over their mouths. The "King" had spoken. No giggles. They'd better obey.

Mrs. Martin served food and more food. Stephanie couldn't finish her second doughnut. Old Sam slurped away at his coffee. It sounded like a sink draining water. It bothered Mrs. Martin but she didn't scold him. He wouldn't pay attention anyway.

Stephanie sat back, full up to her chin. She found herself looking at every part of the kitchen. It was a good place, a good place. The thought kept going around in her head. She could feel herself searching for just the right words to describe it. She could feel herself making it into a picture, a picture of words.

Mrs. Martin stood behind Stephanie and put her hand on her shoulder.

"Honey, you two better go up and get your things packed. Time is flying."

Stephanie glanced quickly at the small clock on the window sill. Was it that time already? She hadn't thought this last morning could go so fast.

She and Rosemary went upstairs, but neither of them talked at first. They sat on the beds for a while. Finally Stephanie pulled out the battered suitcase and began to gather her few things. She wanted to talk but didn't seem to have the right words. There had to be special words for such times but she couldn't find them.

"Do you have your egg? You can't forget that," Rosemary said softly.

Stephanie mumbled yes. She would never leave that behind. First she put it in the corner of the suitcase next to her tennis shoes. That wouldn't do. It might get bumped and broken. She put it back on the bed.

"I wish you could stay," Rosemary said.

"Me too," Stephanie answered in a low voice.

"Did you like it here?"

"Sure." Stephanie really meant that.

"Will you come back during the summer?"

"Could I?" Stephanie asked in surprise. The idea excited her at first. But just as quickly the worry, the trouble about the money for this trip came back to her. She sighed.

"I want you to," Rosemary said, reaching in her pocket.

She took out the little packet her mother had given her from the top of the refrigerator before breakfast.

"I want you to take this home," Rosemary said,

giving it to Stephanie. "Momma said it might not grow but you can try."

The little packet was yellow with one word in big letters along the top. It said "ROSEMARY."

Stephanie smiled. "What is it?" she asked.

"Rosemary is a plant. It grows very tall, Sam says. We can't seem to make it grow here and maybe it won't grow in the city either. But I want you to have it. You can plant it in a can with holes in the bottom for draining. And water it. Not too much, remember. It just might grow for you. Do you want it?"

Stephanie pressed the packet with her fingers. She could feel lumps inside, the seeds of the rosemary plant.

"Yes, I do want it."

"There's something people say about that plant. Momma told me a long time ago. They say 'Rosemary is for remembering.' So that's for you to keep, to remember me."

Stephanie felt some tears again, sad ones mixed with glad ones. Mrs. Martin opened the door just then and smiled.

"We leave soon. Are you ready?"

"She's ready, Momma." Rosemary said. "Do you have that other box for her?"

"Yes, indeed," said Mrs. Martin. She gave Stephanie a cardboard box sealed with tape. It was quite heavy for its size.

"This is soil from Sam's garden. You can put it in a can and use it to plant the rosemary seeds. It won't spill, I sealed it good and tight."

Stephanie tucked the box of dirt in the suitcase and laid the packet of seeds next to it. They closed the suitcase and Stephanie put on her coat. With the white box in her hand, Stephanie followed Mrs. Martin and Rosemary down the stairs. She paused on one step to look back at the room, with its white curtains and blue bows. She would miss it.

Dr. Martin had the car keys jingling from his fist. Sam was in the hall, his soiled hat tucked under his arm. He stuck out his hand.

"Take care of yourself, city gal. Water them seeds three times a week, deep and slow."

So he knew about the rosemary seeds, too. Stephanie thanked him.

Yip and Yap scampered around the porch. Stephanie petted each of them and they licked her fingers. Everyone got in the car, except Sam, who stood on the steps and waved as they drove away.

Stephanie kept looking back. Too quickly the

house disappeared as they wound down the driveway. Rosemary was still talking. She told Stephanie to write and promised to answer. She chattered and made little jokes with her father. But Stephanie didn't have much to say. She held tight to her box with the delicate egg.

In town Dr. Martin parked the car under the same tree where Stephanie had first seen it. The big tree that had looked almost dead just a few days ago had a light coat of green on every branch.

They crossed the road and sat on a wooden bench under the store awning. Dr. Martin talked to some men who drove up in a truck. Mrs. Martin met a friend near the corner and they were busy talking too.

Stephanie and Rosemary were alone for a few minutes.

"Will you come back in the summer?" Rosemary asked again.

"I want to," Stephanie answered. It would be fine to come again. But she couldn't forget how hard it was for her to come this time, how hard it was for her father to get the money in that envelope. She wanted very much to come back but it probably wouldn't happen.

"Remember to water the seeds. It'd be swell if they grew."

"I'll remember," Stephanie promised.

The Red Ridge sign was swinging again and still squeaking on its hinges. The road was quiet, only a few cars around. Mrs. Martin sat with them. Her friend had gone.

"Momma, can Stephanie come back in the summer?" Rosemary asked urgently.

Mrs. Martin rubbed her cheek. She didn't answer right away.

"Well, Honey, we'd love to have her. But we can't plan anything for sure right now. All I can say is that she would be most welcome."

"See?" Rosemary said happily. "You'll be back, I just know it."

There was a rumbling sound far off. It grew louder. Up over a dip in the road came the bus. Stephanie watched it roll toward them. She clutched the white box.

Dr. Martin picked up Stephanie's suitcase. Mrs. Martin held one of her hands and Rosemary put her arms around her. The bus stopped. The door was wide open. The driver was waiting. The people on the bus were waiting, waiting to be on their way, to leave this place called Red Ridge.

And Stephanie cried. She just couldn't help it. Rosemary cried too. They were hanging onto each other. Mrs. Martin whispered to them that the bus was waiting. Dr. Martin went inside and put the suitcase above the seat. But near the bench Stephanie and Rosemary still held hands.

Rosemary whispered in Stephanie's ear, "Please come back. Please, I want you to. Please, Sugar Bee."

Stephanie hugged her again.

"I will. I hope I will," she whispered back. She was glad Rosemary had called her Sugar Bee. It was different now.

Stephanie climbed on the bus and took her seat. Rosemary was still by the bench. Dr. Martin gave the ticket to the driver. They were ready.

Rosemary waved her hand in the air. She was looking straight ahead and not toward the window where Stephanie sat but that was all right. Stephanie waved back.

The bus began to move. It rolled slowly into the wide road and its motor whined. Stephanie sat deep in her seat. She didn't want to see the hills or the trees. She closed her eyes. She could remember Rosemary. Just like people said, "Rosemary is for remembering." She saw the long red hair, the smile, Rosemary waving goodbye.

The white box was in her lap. She opened it again. She wanted to see the lamb. The bus bumped and made it hard to look. But there it was, tiny and white with those blue eyes. It *was* pretty. She would call it "Beautiful."

She gazed out the window. If Rosemary could love something ugly, if Rosemary could find beauty without eyes to see, then she could find beauty too.

It was dark when the bus pulled into the Pittsburgh station. Stephanie was asleep. Her mother's voice wakened her.

"Sugar Bee, wake up. You're home."

She opened her eyes. "Momma!"

Her mother hugged her hard and they left the bus. Her father was waiting for them. He took the suitcase and bent down to hug her.

"Sure good to have you back, Sugar Bee. Did you have a fine time?"

"Yes, Poppa. A fine time."

Hand in hand, the three of them went home.